(If enyone

Finds this book

Phone) 63661

The stories in this book are by:
Margaret Conroy, Gillian Denton, Diane
Jackman, Bob Mathias, Jim Redwood, Sally
Sheringham, Janet Slingsby, Gordon Snell,
Judy Todd, Freda Ward.
The illustrations are by:
Paul Bonner, Tracy Boyd, Sue Cartwright,
David Eaton, Douglas Hall, Robin Lawrie,
Juliana Lea, David Mostyn, John Patience,
Peter Richardson, Yvonne Rothmayr, Margaret
Sherry, Kate Veale, Kay Wilson.

Cover illustration by John Patience

Published 1982 by
The Hamlyn Publishing Group Limited
London · New York · Sydney · Toronto
Astronaut House, Feltham, Middlesex, England
© Copyright The Hamlyn Publishing Group
Limited 1982

ISBN 0 600 36646 4

Printed in Italy

100 STORIES
OF
MANY LANDS

HAMLYN
London · New York · Sydney · Toronto

Contents

In the forest

Kobkua's father worked in the forests of Thailand cutting down trees. Kobkua often watched her father working. She loved to see his elephant lift a heavy tree trunk and trundle it to the river so that it would float down to the sawmill.

Kobkua soon learned the words of command her father used and saw how, as he sat on the elephant's back, he used his knees to tell the elephant what to do.

One night Kobkua's father did not come home. Kobkua went into the forest to look for him, but she found only the elephant. Then she heard a cry for help. She found her father lying beneath a fallen tree.

Kobkua ordered the elephant to kneel. Holding his ear she pulled herself up on his neck. Remembering the words of command, Kobkua made the elephant lift the tree away from her father's leg. Then she rode off to fetch help.

When they heard what had happened the other forest workers ran to carry her father home. His leg was broken, but he was very proud of Kobkua and her skill in handling the elephant. 'My elephant girl,' he said.

The beaver

Long ago in the great forests of Canada the animals held a meeting.

The moose said, 'It is good living in this forest. Our homes are safe.'

The muskrat agreed. 'We have plenty to eat.'

'If only we had water in the hot summer,' said the wolf. 'But then the river runs away into the valley, and there is too little to drink.'

'Perhaps we could catch the river in winter, and keep it somehow,' said the moose.

The animals scratched their heads.

'I think I know what to do,' said the beaver who had been silent until then. He smiled and his big strong teeth flashed in the sunlight.

The beaver began to gnaw round the bottom of a tall tree standing on the riverbank. He gnawed until the tree began to sway from side to side then crash! It fell across the river.

The beaver gnawed at another tree until it too fell across the river with a great crash.

The beaver gnawed and gnawed until the river could no longer run away into the valley. It was trapped behind a wall of trees.

And the next summer the animals had all the water they needed, thanks to the beaver.

Tossing the caber

Rob had been to the Highland Games in Scotland. He enjoyed watching the different sports, but best of all he liked watching the big strong men who tossed the caber, a heavy wooden pole.

At home Rob looked in the garden for a wooden pole, so he could toss the caber too. The first piece of wood he found was the right shape, but too heavy to lift. Then he found a wooden fence-post which was just the right size.

He ran down the lawn and tossed it up in the air with all his strength. It flew over the hedge. Crash! There came the sound of breaking glass.

Rob ran to the hedge and peeped through. The pole had crashed straight through Mr McLeod's greenhouse roof.

Mr McLeod came round to see Rob's parents, but when he heard what Rob had been trying to do, he laughed. 'I used to toss the caber when I was a young man,' he said. 'I'll show you the proper way to do it.'

The cactus flower

Miguel and Carla were walking in the desert near their home in Mexico. On either side of the track many of the cacti were in bloom, their flowers brilliant in the sun. In the distance Miguel spotted a huge cactus with a flower they did not recognize. The children went to have a closer look.

'It's beautiful,' said Carla. 'I've never seen one like that before.' The orange-red flower was like a flaming star with large pointed petals. Later, at home, Miguel and Carla told their family what they had seen.

Their grandmother was very interested. She had a big collection of cacti in pots which she looked after with great care. 'I remember when I was about your age,' she said, 'I saw that cactus flower in the desert, and it has never flowered again from that day to this. You are lucky to have seen it. I only wish I could see it once more.'

'We'll take you tomorrow, Grandmother,' said Miguel. 'You *will* see it again.'

'No,' said his grandmother, 'I am too old to walk so far into the desert, even in the cool of the evening. I must be content with just memories of it.' She looked sad for a moment, thinking back to her childhood.

Miguel and Carla were sorry, too. The next day, as they sat with their paintboxes painting a picture of Navarro, their donkey, Carla had an idea. 'Why don't we paint a picture of the cactus flower for Grandmother?'

The children told their mother what they were going to do and then started out.

When they reached the cactus they spread out their paints and set to work. It was difficult to catch exactly the right shade of reddish-orange, but at last the picture was finished.

That evening when the meal was over Miguel and Carla said to their grandmother, 'We have a surprise for you. Come into the kitchen.'

On the kitchen table lay the picture they had painted for Grandmother – the beautiful cactus flower she thought she would never see again.

'Thank you children,' she said softly, 'I will treasure it always.'

Henry Hippopotamus

Henry Hippopotamus' parents lived beside a deep river in Africa, and Grandpa Hippo lived with them. Every day Mother and Father and Grandpa Hippo swam in the river. They lay in the water, with only their eyes and ears and noses showing, and wallowed happily.

Soon it was Henry's turn to learn to swim. Mother and Father took him to the edge of the water but Henry would not go in.

Mother slid into the water, but Henry stuck his little grey snout in the air and looked the other way.

Father came up behind Henry and tried – very gently – to push him in, but Henry stuck his four feet firmly in the mud and refused to budge.

'I've never heard of a hippopotamus who couldn't swim,' boomed Grandpa Hippo.

'Never mind,' said Mother. 'We'll try again tomorrow.'

So they did, and the next day, and the next. For a whole week they tried, but Henry would not go into the water.

'Everyone will laugh at him,' snorted Grandpa Hippo.

He was right. The monkeys swinging through the trees chattered and giggled. The zebras whinnied down their noses. The water buffalo chuckled deep in their throats. But nothing would make Henry go into the water. He just sat at the edge and watched the rest of his family lazily paddling about.

One day he was sitting on the river-bank all by himself. Mrs Monkey was swinging through the trees with her new baby on her back. She swung down from a very high branch to a very low branch which overhung the river. Crack! The branch snapped. Mrs Monkey grabbed another branch, but her baby slid off her back and fell into the water. 'Help!' shouted Mrs Monkey. 'My baby can't swim.'

Henry looked around. There was no one else about. It was up to him. He jumped into the river with a big splash and kicked his legs. He was swimming! He swam as fast as he could to the little monkey. 'Climb up on my back,' said Henry.

The little monkey scrambled on to Henry's back and he swam quickly to the bank.

Mrs Monkey was overjoyed. 'Thank you, Henry,' she said, 'but I thought you couldn't swim.'

'Not couldn't,' Henry smiled. 'Just wouldn't. But from now on I will. It's great fun.'

Feeding the ducks

Every day Jean-Pierre and his mother went for a walk in the park in the little Belgian town where they lived. Jean-Pierre liked feeding the ducks and listening to the carillon bells. The bells hung in a tall tower in the middle of the park, and each afternoon a man played tunes on them. He played marches and dances and folksongs and Jean-Pierre marched and danced and sang round the park in time with the music.

When the bells stopped, Jean-Pierre still marched and sang. 'What's that tune you're singing?' asked his mother.

'It's called "Feeding the Ducks",' said Jean-Pierre. 'I made it up myself.' And he marched round the lake singing "Feeding the Ducks" at the top of his voice. 'I wish the man in the carillon would play my tune,' he said.

Very soon it was Jean-Pierre's birthday. 'Can we go to the park?' he asked.

Imagine Jean-Pierre's surprise when the first tune he heard from the carillon was "Feeding the Ducks", his very own tune.

But how did the man in the carillon know, he wondered.

Jean-Pierre saw his mother smile. 'Thank you,' he said, hugging her. 'It's the best birthday present ever!'

Magic lanterns

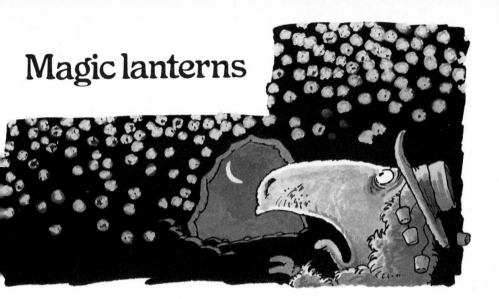

Shirley Sheep lived on a big sheep station in New Zealand. She hated just being an ordinary sheep, she wanted something *exciting* to happen. So, she decided to go on an adventure.

That night, Shirley bravely set off. She'd never set hoof outside the sheep station before and she was a bit frightened – it was very dark and every now and again she heard strange noises.

Eventually she came to a cave. 'That looks a good place to sleep,' she thought, and went in.

Suddenly, she rounded a bend and was surrounded by hundreds of tiny, bluish-green lanterns. Were they magic? 'Is anyone there?' she bleated, very frightened, and instantly all the lanterns went out.

Shirley didn't wait to find out any more. She ran all the way back to the sheep station where, breathlessly, she told the others about the magic lanterns.

All the sheep roared with laughter. 'They weren't magic lanterns,' said one. 'They were glow-worms!'

Shirley felt rather foolish. But the glow-worms had given her such a fright that they'd put her off adventures for good.

Soo-Ling sees a panda

Soo-Ling was looking for pandas. Although she had searched in the bamboo forest near her home in western China many times, she had never seen one. Years ago there had been pandas near her home, but they had moved deeper into the forest away from people.

Suddenly she caught sight of something moving among the bamboo. Soo-Ling could not believe it at first. Then she saw it clearly – a giant panda chewing quietly at a tough bamboo stem.

Excitedly she rushed to tell her parents who were working

in the fields outside the village.

'I've just seen a panda!' she cried.

'There haven't been any pandas around here since I was a boy,' said her father.

'I did see it,' insisted Soo-Ling. 'Perhaps the pandas will come back now and we shall have a whole family living in the forest.'

But Soo-Ling's words had been overheard by Wang, a greedy man who saw a way to make some money. If there was a panda in the forest, he would capture it and sell it.

With the help of his two evil sons, Wang set out that night for the forest.

Soo-Ling lay awake thinking about the panda. Tomorrow she would look again to make sure she had not been mistaken. Footsteps passed her house and she heard a muffled cough. She looked out of the window and saw three men leaving the village with nets and sticks.

Quietly she slipped out of the house after them. As she drew closer she heard them talking about the panda. Dismayed, Soo-Ling ran home to wake her father.

'All I ever hear about is pandas,' said Soo-Ling's father sleepily. But he dressed quickly and woke some of his neighbours. Together they followed Soo-Ling to the place where she had seen the panda that morning.

Wang and his sons had set the net and were waiting, hidden among the bamboo stems.

The panda appeared in the clearing and began to wander towards the net. In an instant Soo-Ling's father picked up a rock and threw it into the net. The trap sprang and the net fell harmlessly to the ground.

Wang and his sons realized that they had been caught out and ran away, never to be seen in the village again.

And the pandas did come back and lived undisturbed in the bamboo forest.

The magic goblet

Henrik was a poor forester in Norway, and lived in a little cabin beside a lake. He often looked up at the mountains on the far side of the water, and thought about the legend of the troll. This troll was supposed to live in a cave in the mountains, and the legend said that he had a magic silver goblet.

Henrik decided to try and find the troll. If he could get the magic goblet it would grant all his wishes.

He made a special pair of wooden skis, slid carefully across the frozen lake, and began to climb up the snowy slopes of the mountains.

When he was nearly at the top and was beginning to think there was no such thing as a troll, he saw a cave and, just as he reached the cave, the troll's crafty old face peered out of the entrance, smiling.

Henrik was scared, but the troll said, 'Welcome, Henrik. How kind of you to come and see me. Would you like a drink? You must be thirsty.'

'Well, th . . . thank you,' said Henrik, nervously.

'Wait here.' The troll went into the cave, and came back carrying the silver goblet. He handed it to Henrik. It was full of a dark bubbling liquid. Henrik raised the goblet towards his mouth, then suddenly felt fearful. He flung his arm into the air, and the liquid in the goblet flew over his shoulder. Henrik looked round, and saw that it had melted a big patch of snow into steam.

The troll cackled, and leaped at Henrik, but he zoomed off down the slopes on his skis, clutching the goblet.

'I'll soon catch you!' snarled the troll. 'Just wait till I put on my magic bouncing trousers!'

He pulled on a pair of baggy red trousers and started to bounce down the mountain.

Henrik slid down the slopes as fast as he could, but every
time he looked round, the bouncing troll was catching him
up. When he reached the lake, the troll was just behind him.
Henrik jumped sideways, and fell down in the snow.

The troll couldn't stop himself. He bounced on to the ice
of the lake. Bump, bump, bump, bump, and then – crash,
splash! The ice broke, and the troll disappeared into the
chilly water with a scream. Henrik waited, but he didn't
come up. There was only a sizzle of steam, rising from the
hole in the ice. . . .

Henrik went home, holding the silver goblet and thinking
of all the wishes he would make.

The reed boat

Juan and Manuel were playing by the shore of the great Lake Titicaca in Peru. 'My uncle told me I could use his boat,' said Manuel. 'It's further down the shore.'

The two boys went to find it. 'Is this the right boat?' asked Juan, looking at the broken bundles of reeds which made up the boat. 'It doesn't look safe.'

'Of course it is,' said Manuel, jumping on the boat and pushing off. The boat moved slowly and heavily out into the lake. Then it began to turn in circles. One end was sinking!

Juan ran down the shore towards some fishermen's huts to fetch help. On the way he noticed a new boat tied up. He dragged it into the water and paddled hard towards Manuel. He reached his friend just as one end of the old boat slipped underwater.

'Take hold of the paddle,' he shouted and Manuel jumped across safely.

They reached the shore as Manuel's uncle came up. 'Have you had a good time?' he asked.

'Is this your boat?' gasped Manuel. 'I took the old boat.'

'That old boat was dangerous,' said his uncle. 'They don't last long. I'm glad Juan found my new boat in time.'

The leprechaun

In Ireland, nestled where the mountains sweep down towards the sea, lay a group of tiny, white cottages.

Bronagh lived here. She was a little girl with eyes as green and beautiful as the land around her. One day she was searching the hillside for a shamrock, for tomorrow was St Patrick's Day, and to wear a shamrock then was very lucky. But she couldn't find one anywhere. She flopped on the grass and sighed.

'Help!' squeaked a voice. 'You're sitting on me!' Bronagh jumped up. She saw a little tiny man dressed all in green. 'A leprechaun!' she gasped.

He nodded. 'And my foot is caught on a root,' he squeaked. 'If you free me, you can have a share of my crock of gold!'

Bronagh pulled the roots and freed him. 'I don't want your fairy-gold,' she said, 'but I do want a shamrock, so I can wear it tomorrow.'

The leprechaun pointed to a crooked tree. 'You'll find your shamrock under there, now and every year. But never tell, or it will not grow again.' Then he was gone.

And for ever after, people wondered how Bronagh always had a lucky shamrock to wear on St Patrick's Day.

The strange buffalo

It was a cold, cold winter and the Indian tribe shivered in its tepees on the plains of North America. They were cold and hungry because the great herds of buffalo which once roamed across the plains had gone.

'What shall we do without the buffalo?' Running Deer asked his father, Chief Red Eagle.

'We need the buffalo meat for food, and we need their skins to make clothing. Without them we cannot go on living here. We shall have to move to new hunting grounds,' his father replied.

The whole tribe was troubled. No one wanted to leave the lands where the tribe had lived for as long as stories had been told.

Running Deer mounted his pony and rode out across the plain. It was growing dark, and as the moon rose slowly, casting its pale light on the ground, Running Deer thought he glimpsed a glint of silver.

He rubbed his eyes. Sometimes they played strange tricks on him, especially when he was hungry.

He saw the glint of silver again and rode towards it. Where the moonbeams touched the earth, Running Deer saw a buffalo standing in a pool of light. Its horns were of silver and shone brilliantly through the darkness.

As Running Deer drew nearer, the buffalo turned towards

24

a range of hills far away across the plain. Running Deer
followed. All night long they travelled and reached the
lower slopes of the hills just as the sun rose.

Surefooted, the buffalo scrambled up a steep, narrow
track which disappeared between the rocks.

Running Deer and his pony had difficulty keeping up.
But at last the buffalo stood on the top ridge of the hills, its
horns now pale gold in the rays of the weak winter sun.

When Running Deer reached the ridge and looked down
into the valley, he could hardly believe his eyes. The valley
was covered with thousands upon thousands of buffalo,
quietly grazing. It was the biggest herd he had ever seen.

'Thank you,' he called softly to the magic buffalo. 'Thank
you for bringing me here. Now our tribe will not have to
leave its lands. There will be food enough for us for ever.'

25

The dancing bear

Jan warmed his hands at the fire his grandfather had made.
It was growing dark and out on the wild Yugoslavian
mountains the wind howled and growled.

Jan shivered. The howling, growling noise grew louder.
'What's that, Grandfather?' he said. 'Do you think it's a
wolf or a bear? Or perhaps it's only the wind?'

'Don't worry, Jan,' said Grandfather. 'You'll be quite safe
with me. Look, I've brought my gusla in case the bears
come to dance.'

He opened his bag and took out a wooden musical
instrument with only one string. Grandfather softly plucked
the string and played a merry tune. 'Did I ever tell you,' he
said, 'about the time I camped on the mountain when I was
a boy? It was dark and cold and through the trees I heard a
growling, howling noise.'

'Something like that?' whispered Jan as he heard the
noise again.

'I looked around,' said Grandfather, 'but I could see

nothing so I lay down to sleep. Suddenly I woke up again. The growling was close at hand. Into the circle of fire-light lumbered an enormous bear. It snuffled round the fire and came nearer and nearer.'

'Were you frightened, Grandfather?' asked Jan.

'Very. I had no weapons. I stretched out my hand and picked up my gusla. As I did my finger plucked the string, and at the first note the bear stood on its hind legs. I started to play a sad little tune I knew. The bear moved slowly about. Then I played a dance and the bear began to hop up and down and twirl round to the music of the dance.'

Jan's eyes grew wider. 'Really, Grandfather? What happened then?'

'I kept playing,' replied his grandfather. 'I played faster and faster. The faster I played, the faster the bear danced. He danced and danced round the fire, and finally he danced through the trees and I was alone again.'

'What a lucky escape,' breathed Jan.

'And that is why I always bring my gusla with me on the mountain,' said Grandfather, 'in case the bears come to dance.'

27

Beating the drum

Mr Ndongo had so many children that he had to build another hut for his big family. All the other families in the African village sent someone to help him.

Matthew beat a drum. 'This helps everyone to work together,' he explained to his little sister Mary, 'and then the work is finished quickly.'

Boom, boom, boom went the drum.

Slap, slap, slap went everyone's hands slapping the clay into a round wall.

When the wall was dry the men made ropes of reeds from the river to tie the roof poles together. 'Come and help us, Matthew,' they called, 'we need another pair of hands.'

To Mary's delight Matthew gave her the drum. 'You beat the drum, while I help the men.'

Boom, boom, boom Mary beat steadily.

Then the men were ready to cover the roof with more reeds to keep out the rain.

'I'll carry on with the roof,' said Matthew, 'and you beat the drum. You're very good.'

So Mary beat the drum till the work was finished.

The hula-hula pig

On a small Hawaiian island lived a wild pig called Kokua
who wanted, more than anything, to be a hula-hula dancer.
Every evening she would hide behind a palm tree and watch
the dancers. They wore skirts made of tapa leaves and
garlands of flowers, called leis, round their necks.

'How beautiful they look,' thought Kokua. 'And how I
wish I could join in.' But no one would ever allow a *pig* to
dance!

Then one day Kokua overheard the dancers say that one
of the girls was ill and wouldn't be able to dance that
evening. It was an important night, too, as lots of tourists
were coming to watch.

This was Kokua's chance! She crept to the hut where the
dancers kept their costumes, and there hung the spare skirt
and garland. She slipped them on. The skirt just fitted
round her rather plump waist. After admiring herself in the
mirror, she went and joined the dancers on the seashore.

Everyone roared with laughter when they saw Kokua. But
when the tourists saw what an excellent dancer she was, they
stopped laughing and clapped instead, and they took lots of
photographs. What a thing to show the folks back home – a
pig hula-hula dancer!

Boomerang practice

In the bushlands of Australia, live the native aborigines. They live a gypsy life, travelling from one water-hole to another, searching for food. They build shelters with poles covered with tree bark, and hunt with long spears and boomerangs.

Nimmo was a small aborigine boy. One day his father said to him, 'You are now old enough to begin hunting. First, you must be able to use a weapon,' and he gave him a boomerang.

Boomerangs are curved weapons. When thrown cleverly, they come back to the thrower. Nimmo was pleased with his new boomerang. But his father warned him, 'Not until you can catch it properly, will I teach you to hunt.'

Then he and the other men and older boys, set off for the day's hunting.

Nimmo took his boomerang a long way into the bush, to practise. He threw the boomerang around all day. First it stuck in a tree. Then it went high up in the sky and tangled with a bird. Next it bounced along the ground. Then he flung it, and a rabbit got in the way. In fact it did everything except return for him to catch it.

In the end, he became upset. Not once could he catch the boomerang, it always hit something instead of returning to him!

Near to tears, he gathered up everything the boomerang had struck, and dragged them wearily back to camp.

His father had just returned. He was in a bad temper, because the hunt had been a failure. Nimmo's knees shook. Bravely he went up to him.

'I'm no good,' he said sadly, handing his father the boomerang. 'I can't catch it, no matter how hard I try.'

'What's that?' asked his father, staring. Nimmo gulped.

'What's that?' he asked again. Suddenly Nimmo realized
that his father meant the things he was holding. Nimmo
showed him. 'I just kept hitting things,' he said, putting
down the various animals, birds and lizards. Everyone
gathered round and stared.

Then his father began to laugh. 'We have some food,
after all!' he cried, wiping his eyes. He put Nimmo on his
knee. 'My son,' he said, 'catching food is more important
than catching boomerangs! You have hunted better than
anyone today. From now on, you hunt with us!'

Nimmo gave a big, beaming smile.

At the bazaar

'Jamshed,' his mother said, 'you must take the goat into town to sell. There is no other way for us to get the money we need to pay the rent.' Jamshed's mother was sorry to lose their fine goat, but there was nothing else she could think of to sell.

Jamshed tied a rope around the goat's neck and set off on his long walk. The track was dusty and stony, but at last he reached the busy little town in Pakistan.

'I'll go into the bazaar while I am here,' he thought. Jamshed did not often go to the town, so it was a treat for him to wander round the bazaar, even on such a sad day as this. He loved the sights and sounds of the bazaar and the little stalls selling everything from bright woven carpets to tiny cups of hot, fragrant tea. One man was selling delicious smelling dishes of spicy food which made Jamshed feel hungry.

Still leading the goat through the jostling people he moved on towards a man playing his pipe over a basket of snakes.

Suddenly he heard shouts of 'Stop thief!' A man in blue was running towards Jamshed, pushing his way roughly through the crowds. He kept his hand hidden inside his short coat.

Jamshed stepped back and jerked on the rope round his goat's neck. The rope pulled tight. The man tripped over it and fell sprawling on the ground.

'Well done, boy,' said the stall-keeper who had been chasing the thief. He seized the arm of the man lying on the ground and shook him. 'Give me back the bracelet!' he said sharply.

The man in blue took his hand from his short coat. He held a heavy gold bracelet, skilfully worked in beautiful patterns and studded with precious stones.

'That is the finest piece of jewellery I have for sale,' said the stall-keeper. 'This thief knew which one to steal.'

He turned to Jamshed. 'Come with me. You shall have a reward for your quick action.'

When Jamshed saw the generous reward the stall-keeper had given him he was overjoyed. 'Now I shan't have to sell our goat,' he said. 'My mother will be so pleased when she sees me bringing the goat home again.'

The grapes

Kara lived on the warm island of Cyprus, where long beaches are washed by sunlit seas, and grapes grow in the foothills to make sweet wine. Kara's mother worked in the vineyards, and Kara usually went too. She rode to the vineyards on their donkey and played with her friends among the vines while her mother picked the grapes.

Her mother would pick from the vines, then empty her basket into large panniers strapped to the donkey's sides.

Each day Kara's father asked, 'Have you done well today?', and her mother would answer, 'Yes!' But one day, she said, 'No!' For suddenly, the panniers seemed to take much longer to fill, no matter how hard she picked.

Kara's father was angry. 'Someone is stealing your grapes instead of working!' he cried. 'Tomorrow I will come and see who it can be!' So the next day, he hid himself, and watched. And he couldn't believe his eyes.

For, as Kara's mother filled the panniers, naughty Kara and her friends ate the grapes!

After that, Kara and the other children were made to help with the grape harvest. But they didn't mind. It was fun picking grapes and you could always eat a few as you picked!

The scruffy penguin

The penguins at the South Pole always looked very smart
with their neat black backs and spotless white fronts. But to
stay neat and spotless the penguins had to spend a lot of
time preening and cleaning.

Apart from Peter. Peter liked to roll down the beach and
jump into the sea and splash about and have fun.

The other penguins thought Peter was scruffy. 'He's
covered in seaweed,' said one. 'I can see fishbones in his
feathers,' said another.

Peter didn't care. 'I'm having fun,' he said. Then one
day, when the sea was still like a looking-glass, Peter caught
sight of himself. His feathers were crumpled, his white front
was green with seaweed and a fishbone stuck out of his tail.
He jumped into the sea – thinking hard.

One of the smart penguins saw him and sighed, 'Peter may
be scruffy, but he does have fun.' The other penguins
cleaned their feathers again – thinking hard.

When Peter climbed out of the sea, he began to preen
and clean himself, for the first time. But just as he put the
last feather in place, the other penguins rolled past and
splashed into the sea, and began to have fun, for the first
time.

Anansi the spider

Anansi the Spider was at the king's palace one day, boasting
about his bravery. 'You know Leopard who lives near my
home in the forest? Well, I can ride about on his back, like
a cowboy on a horse.'

'I'll believe that when I see it,' laughed the king. And
next time Leopard called at the palace, he asked if what
Anansi said was true.

Leopard was very angry. 'It's a lie,' he cried. 'And I'll
make Anansi admit it. I'll bring him here to confess to you
himself.'

He hurried away into the forest, and knocked on the
hollow tree where Anansi lived. 'Come with me to the king,
Anansi, and confess you lied, when you said I let you ride
on my back.'

Anansi appeared at his entrance-hole. 'I would love to come, Leopard,' he said, 'but I'm not feeling well. I'm not strong enough to walk. If you'll carry me to the palace, I'll certainly confess.'

'Oh, all right,' said Leopard. 'As long as you tell the king the truth.'

'Of course,' said Anansi, 'but I'm so weak, I'm afraid I'll slip off your back. I'll have to have a saddle, and a bridle, and reins to hold on to.'

'All right, but hurry,' said Leopard, as Anansi put a saddle on his back, and a bridle round his head.

'There's just one more thing,' said Anansi. 'The flies are very bad today. I'll take this whip, so that I can swish them away when they buzz round me.'

'Oh, stop dithering,' said Leopard. 'Take your silly whip, and get on my back.'

Anansi climbed into the saddle, and Leopard ran through the forest. As they got near the palace, Anansi saw that the king was sitting on his porch, enjoying the sunshine.

'Look, Your Majesty!' shouted Anansi, and he began to crack the whip and call out, 'Giddy-up, Leopard. Giddy-up, Leopard. Faster, boy, faster!'

Leopard stopped in front of the king, and Anansi said: 'Am I not riding Leopard just as I told you?'

'You certainly are,' said the king, chuckling.

The cream castle

Franz and Liesl sat in a café, in a little town in Austria, eating Mr Grunwald's delicious cakes. 'You look sad today, Mr Grunwald,' said Liesl. 'What is wrong?'

'I do not have enough customers,' replied the old man. 'Most people go to the big café in the main square for their coffee and cakes. They don't seem to find this little side street. So, I must close my café.'

Sadly Franz and Liesl finished their cakes and went into the main square. A man was nailing a large notice to one of the trees. There was to be a big competition to make a model of Klosberg Castle.

Klosberg Castle stood on a hill outside the town. It was a

beautiful castle with lots of round towers and high walls with tiny pointed windows.

'It wouldn't be easy to make a model of the castle,' said Liesl.

Franz agreed. 'But I've an idea. Let's go back and see Mr Grunwald about it.'

On the morning of the competition Franz and Liesl called at Mr Grunwald's little café. 'Is it ready?' they asked.

'I have been working on it all night,' said Mr Grunwald. 'Come and look.'

On the table in the kitchen stood a model of Klosberg Castle. The walls and towers were made of cake and the whole castle was beautifully iced and decorated with cream and chocolate.

'It's wonderful,' said Franz.

'It's like a fairytale castle,' said Liesl. 'You are clever, Mr Grunwald.'

Very carefully they carried the cake up the street to the main square and into the Town Hall. The building was filled with models of Castle Klosberg – in clay, in wood, in stone, in paper, even in matchsticks.

While the judges decided, everyone had to wait outside in the square. At last the Mayor came out and announced, 'The winner is Mr Grunwald with his castle of cake and whipped cream.'

He presented Mr Grunwald with the prize and everyone clapped and cheered before going into the Town Hall to have another look at the wonderful cake castle.

Mr Grunwald was delighted, and when he went home he found a long queue of people waiting outside his café. Everyone wanted to try some of his famous cakes.

Now Mr Grunwald's little café is always busy, but Liesl and Franz know that Mr Grunwald keeps a table in the corner specially for them.

At the oasis

Nessim was very excited. This was the first time he had been allowed to journey into the great Saudi Arabian desert with his father. But it was very hot and he was glad when they stopped to rest at an oasis where there were palm trees and a pool.

His father nodded off to sleep, and Nessim wandered away into the desert. In the distance, he saw hazy shapes that seemed to shimmer, like reflections in water. They looked like palm trees beside a big lake. Nessim walked towards them. He walked and walked, but they never got any nearer.

It was very, very hot, and he felt dizzy, and sat down. His throat was as dry as dust, and his skin felt as if it was burning. He tried to stand up, but he felt too faint.

Then he heard the voice of his father, who had come to find him. He carried Nessim back to the oasis, and explained that the palm trees and the lake in the distance were not real – they were called a 'mirage', a trick of the light that often happens in deserts.

Theresa's picnic

Theresa was excited because today all the families from the farms in the Spanish valley where she lived would climb the hill for the grand picnic.

Theresa collected a bundle of sticks, her mother packed a big basket of food and her father carried it all up the hill.

In a shady spot Father lit the fire while Mother unpacked the rice and fish and chicken and vegetables to make paella.

Suddenly Mother exclaimed, 'I've forgotten the cooking pot. What shall we do!'

Just then a hat came rolling past. Theresa caught it. 'I'll go and see whose hat this is,' she said.

Further up the path an old man and his wife were sitting by a cooking pot. 'You've found my hat,' said the old man. 'Many thanks. Are you enjoying the picnic?'

Theresa told them about the cooking pot.

'Please use ours,' said the old lady. 'Our soup is almost ready.'

Mother was delighted to see the cooking pot. 'Would those kind people like to picnic with us?' she said. Theresa hurried back to invite them.

When the meal was over, the old man played folksongs on his guitar and everyone gathered around their fire and sang and danced until nightfall.

The boat race

Abi lived in a village on the edge of the sea in Papua New Guinea. In fact the village was actually in the sea! The houses were perched on stilts above the water and when Abi wanted to visit her friends she had to walk along wooden planks between the houses. When she wanted a bath, all she had to do was jump straight out of the house and into the sea.

One morning Abi had a particularly good wash in the sea for today was the day of the boat race and in the evening there would be dancing and storytelling. She put on the traditional costume of the island – a grass skirt and beautiful necklaces of beads and shells. In her hair she put a headdress made of feathers.

As soon as she was ready she ran down to the shore where the boats were being made ready for the great race. The boats were called lakatois and were like two canoes bound together. Each boat had a sail.

Abi looked around for her father. He and some of his friends were taking part in the race and Abi wanted to wish them good luck. When her father saw her he picked her up and whirled her around. 'You look beautiful in your costume,' he said. 'How would you like to sail with us in the race to bring us good luck?'

Abi couldn't believe it was true. None of the other children were allowed to go and she was so pleased she could hardly keep still. But her father said that once they were in the boat she must be very still and quiet or she would spoil their chances of winning.

Abi was so busy watching the other boats and keeping out of everyone's way that the race seemed to be over as soon as it had begun. Their boat came second and Abi was a bit disappointed but her father was really pleased. 'Next year we will be first,' he said.

And when Abi got back on to the shore she found everyone dancing and singing. All her friends were dressed in traditional costume too and they pulled Abi into the dance. By the time the sun was setting Abi was worn out. She was glad to sit around the fire and listen to stories of long ago.

The wish

'Gosh, it's so hot,' said Dominique as she lounged on the verandah of her grandfather's house. 'I really do wish it would rain.' She squinted up into the bright summer-blue sky.

Dominique's grandfather rocked backwards and forwards in his old chair. All around him was the soft summer buzz of insects. He tilted his white floppy hat down low over his eyes. 'Never wish for the weather to change,' he said. 'You must let it decide for itself.'

Dominique, who thought her grandfather was asleep, was startled, then puzzled. She sat up and wrapped her hands around her knees. 'Why do you say that, Grandfather?' she asked.

The old man sat up. 'When I was a boy,' he began, 'I lived by a great river. I believed then that it went right around the world. It was called the Marne and it travelled right across France.' He paused and shifted in his chair.

'One very hot day, just like today,' he went on, 'I wished for rain, just like you.' The old man's blue eyes twinkled. 'No sooner had I made my wish than it started to rain. It rained all day and all night, on and on and on, it seemed to go on forever. The great river rose higher and higher and finally it broke its banks and flooded the land, including my father's fields.'

The old man leant forward and his voice dropped to a whisper. 'I thought it was my fault. I thought my father would be cross with me. I wished and wished for the rain to stop but it was no good, the water came right up to the door of my father's house. Only then did it stop.'

Dominique laughed. 'Were you very frightened, Grandfather?' she asked, smiling up at the old man.

'Yes I was, but I don't think my father really blamed me.' The old man chuckled to himself at the memory.

'So wishes don't really come true, after all,' said Dominique, smiling.

'Ah,' said the old man, 'but after that terrible flood I have never risked wishing for the weather to change again – just in case!'

The pumpkins

'Please may I have a pumpkin to make a lantern for the Hallowe'en party?' asked Jim.

'Don't forget Mother needs three for her special American pumpkin pies,' said his father.

In the garden Jim found four large pumpkins. 'Three for Mother, one for me,' thought Jim.

He sliced off the top and scooped out the soft inside leaving only the pumpkin shell. On the front he cut two round holes for eyes, a triangle for a nose and a square for a mouth. It looked very fierce, especially when the candle inside the lantern was lit.

Jim left it on the wall to dry. But he didn't know that Mr Benson's goat, Abner, was loose in the yard next door. Abner would eat anything. Newspapers, gardening gloves, Mrs Benson's geraniums. The sight of Jim's pumpkin was too much for Abner. He took a big bite. Mmmmm.

When Jim came out to fetch his lantern, only the half-chewed candle lay on the wall.

Mr Benson was very sorry when he heard what Abner had done. He took Jim to his vegetable patch and let him pick the biggest pumpkin he could find.

'I'll keep it out of Abner's reach this time,' said Jim.

The book fair

Every year in the town of Bologna in Italy there was a
Children's Book Fair. On the last day the children of the
town were allowed in to see all the books on display.

Rico and Anna went with their mother, and as they
entered they came to a stand decorated just like a fairy
palace. Large figures made of cardboard stood right along
the front. There were soldiers, wizards, knights and
princesses. The two children looked longingly at the tall
figures and the salesman in charge smiled quietly to
himself.

The next morning, when they woke, they were surprised
to see the figures from the fair leaning along the front wall
of their garden. Rico spotted a note pinned to one of the
figures. 'We are for you,' he said, reading it to Anna. 'The
fair is now over, so please can you look after us very
carefully.' And there was a book with stories all about these
magic people.

Rico and Anna laughed happily as they carried the
brightly coloured figures into their house. They were sorry
they couldn't thank the kind salesman but they certainly
would thank him next year. And they were really looking
forward to reading all the stories.

Tanku the monkey

Deep in the Malaysian jungle lived a family of pig-tailed monkeys. They were all very happy except for the youngest monkey, whose name was Tanku. For Tanku was bored living in the damp, gloomy jungle day after day. He longed to see what life was like outside. So, on one particularly boring day, he decided to run away. That night, when all was quiet, he made his getaway, nimbly swinging along creepers and branches.

It was still dark when he reached the edge of the jungle. So he curled up and slept. What a sight met his eyes when he awoke! And what a racket! Horns were blaring and cars and motor-cycles were racing along the road, and there were people everywhere. Tanku had certainly never seen anything like this in the jungle!

He was just beginning to think that maybe he liked the jungle best, after all, when a van squealed to a halt beside him. The driver stuck his arm through the window and grabbed Tanku. The next thing Tanku knew, he was inside the van and being driven along at fast speed.

The man said, 'You're going to pick coconuts for me,

Monkey, and if I ever see you slacking I shall get very cross.'
And so the man taught Tanku to climb up coconut palms,
pick coconuts and drop them into a basket below. At first he
often missed the basket but after a time he became a very
good shot.

But Tanku wasn't at all happy with his new life. The work
was hard and his owner didn't give him enough food. At
night he was locked up in a cage. How he longed for the
peace and quiet of the jungle. But how could he escape?

A few days later, Tanku, looking down from the top of a
coconut palm, saw his owner reading a newspaper in the sun.
Suddenly he had an idea. He picked the largest coconut he
could find and dropped it, not into the basket, but crash! On
to his owner's head!

Tanku didn't wait to find out what happened. Quickly he
swung from palm to palm until he was back on that same
road where his adventure had begun. And there, ahead of
him, was the jungle. By nightfall, he was back safe and sound
with his family. He certainly would never leave the jungle
again, unless he had a *very* good reason.

The puppet show

Alexander looked out of the window as big snowflakes began to fall. 'I hope it stops soon,' he said, 'or we won't reach the town to see Mr Popov's Travelling Puppet Show.'

The sky was grey and heavy. The snow fell faster and the wind blew hard. Alexander's father came in from the farm. 'There'll be no puppet show for us tonight,' he said. 'The wind has driven the snow into a big wall across the road to town.'

Alexander was very disappointed because Mr Popov's Puppet Show came to the little Russian town for only one night each year.

Alexander and his parents were sitting down to their evening meal when they heard lorries driving into the yard. Alexander's father went outside to see what was happening. He came in with four people. 'It's Mr Popov and his friends,' he said.

Alexander's mother gave them a hot drink and some food while Mr Popov explained. 'We found the road to the town was blocked. There'll be no show tonight.'

'We couldn't get to the show either,' said Alexander.

'Perhaps we can do something about that,' said Mr Popov and he whispered something to Alexander's father.

'What a good idea,' Father replied. 'I'll go and tell everyone.' When he got back he said to Alexander, 'Will you take Mr Popov to the barn and give him any help he needs?'

Alexander was puzzled, but he showed Mr Popov the barn. The men began to unload big packing cases from the lorries. Alexander saw curtains and scenery and last of all, a huge wicker basket full of puppets! Like magic, the barn was changed into a theatre.

'Now we need seats,' said Mr Popov. 'Could we borrow a few chairs from the house?'

Alexander ran backwards and forwards carrying chairs, but when the people from the village began to arrive at the barn, there weren't enough seats. So Alexander and his father fetched sacks and bales for them to sit on.

The show began. The puppets danced and sang in their bright costumes. Everyone clapped and cheered, and afterwards the children were allowed to work the puppets. It was very difficult and the strings kept tangling.

'You must practise,' said Mr Popov, 'for years and years and years!'

Alexander made up his mind to do just that.

The hidden track

Walking up to the old mine the summer visitors waved to Megan sitting on her garden wall. They came from the valley on a narrow gauge railway train, but halfway up the steep Welsh mountainside the track stopped. Everyone had to walk the rest of the way.

'I wish the trains went all the way to the mine,' Megan said to Mr Jones, the train driver. 'They would steam right past our house.'

'When I was a boy the track did go to the mine,' said Mr Jones.

When Megan heard this she decided to look for the old railway track. She explored everywhere and was just thinking it was teatime, when she tripped over something. Hidden in the long grass lay a length of rusty iron track. She followed it all the way to the old mine workings.

'Perhaps the line could be opened again,' she said to Mr Jones, showing him the track the next day.

And it was. For the rest of the year people were hard at work mending the track and making it safe.

So the following summer Megan was able to wave to the visitors on the train as it steamed past her garden wall.

The magical tea-plant

Long ago on the island of Sri Lanka lived an Emperor who loved tea. His servants knew many secret recipes and visiting princes marvelled at the wonderful tea they were offered.

One day the Emperor pushed aside his seventeenth cup of tea. 'Bring me something new!' he ordered.

But no one could find a new tea to please him. Finally the Emperor offered a sack of gold to the person who found him a delicious new tea.

Far from the palace lived Sula and her grandmother. In their garden grew the most fragrant tea-plant in the world, but they would not sell it, even for a sack of gold.

Two thieves heard of their tea-plant and plotted to steal it. Early one morning they secretly dug up the tea-plant and fled back to the city leaving behind nothing but a single leaf.

Sula and her grandmother wept, and where their tears fell on the leaf, a new tea-plant sprang up.

The thieves did not win the sack of gold, for the stolen tea-plant withered and died in the strange soil.

But each year Sula and her grandmother sent enough tea from their magical tea-plant for the Emperor to have two cups of fragrant tea on his birthday.

Orange picking

The old town of Jaffa is in Israel. Jaffa has mosques, dome-roofed houses and some of the narrowest of streets and stairways. Near the town are many orange groves.

One holidaytime, Nurit gathered her brothers and sisters around her. 'Soon,' she said, 'it will be Grandfather's birthday. I think we should buy him a new hookah pipe.'

'With what?' asked David, her eldest brother. 'We haven't any money.'

'I know,' nodded Nurit. 'But there are six of us, and between us we should be able to earn enough.'

'Me earn,' said Rachel, her baby sister.

David looked at her in dismay. 'But what can we do which includes the little ones?'

'We will work in the orange groves!' answered Nurit. So they walked, in a line, through Jaffa, and down to the orange groves. There, they were given wooden buckets to put the oranges in. The man laughed at them, saying, 'I can't see you children gathering many.'

But they tried. They filled the buckets, then emptied them into a large, wooden crate. At the end of an hour, they were hot, thirsty, and nowhere near to filling one crate. Rachel had given up long ago, and was sitting down sucking an orange.

'This won't do,' sighed Nurit. 'The buckets are too heavy.'

Then she had an idea, and, as they rested awhile, she explained her plan to her brothers and sisters.

When they began picking again, the man stared in astonishment. For the children were in a line, from the orange trees to the crate, and not using a bucket at all! Nurit picked an orange, then it was passed right down the line to Rachel, who popped it into the crate with glee.

Soon, they had filled enough crates for the money they needed.

They all ran back to Jaffa, to the street market, which sells everything you can think of. The children had a lovely time wandering around and choosing a hookah pipe for their grandfather. When they had bought it, they found that they had a little money left over. Enough to buy a large glass of 'mitz' each, which is – fresh orange-juice!

The Greek statue

A very long time ago, a boy called Stephano lived in the Greek town of Delphi. It was a most beautiful place, set amongst the olive groves of Mount Parnassus; it was also a holy place where the sun god Apollo was worshipped. Stephano loved living there.

He was the youngest son of the village innkeeper and he worked very hard every day, helping his father and mother in their inn. He collected the hens' eggs and milked the goats and gathered herbs and swept the floors. But every afternoon when the sun was very hot, Stephano's father and mother went to sleep under the shade of the vines, and Stephano climbed the slopes of Mount Parnassus to a little white building set amongst the trees.

In the little building worked Stephano's friend, the sculptor Demetrius. Stephano loved to visit him, for his little studio was filled with pots and brushes and dyes, and lumps of marble and clay. Demetrius would work with little hammers and chisels to make beautiful statues.

'What are you working on today, Demetrius?' Stephano asked one blazing afternoon.

Demetrius smiled. 'I'm about to start something I've wanted to do for a very long time,' and he showed Stephano many drawings of a young man driving a chariot. Even in the drawings Stephano could see that the man was very powerful and had shining eyes. 'I'm going to make him in bronze,' said Demetrius.

Stephano visited Demetrius every day, and gradually the charioteer took shape before his eyes. When it was finished, Stephano thought the tall bronze man and his chariot was the most beautiful statue he had ever seen.

'You must give him to Apollo,' he said.

'I shall,' said Demetrius, 'and people from all over Greece will come to see him.'

More than two thousand years have passed since that time, and the temples have crumbled, but the charioteer still stands at Delphi, and people come to see him from all over the world.

The koala bear

Patti and her twin brother Paul lived in Australia. One day Patti came running to find her brother. 'Paul,' she cried, 'guess what I've found. It's grey and white, with big cheeks, and a nose like a leather button!'

'It sounds like a koala bear,' said Paul. 'Where is it – can I come and see it?'

They both ran up the dusty track, then Patti stopped. 'Under here!' she whispered, and from a bush lifted out a tiny baby koala bear, which snuggled into her arms.

'Poor thing,' said Patti, cuddling him. 'He must be hungry.' So they took the baby koala back to the house to feed him.

They tried him with milk. They tried him with honey. They tempted him with everything they could think of, but the little bear would not eat or drink!

At last Daddy came home, and when they told him about the koala, he laughed, and said, 'Koala bears only eat the leaves of the eucalyptus tree. "Koala" means "no drink" – the leaves are food and drink to a koala!'

'Ugh,' said Patti. 'I'm glad I'm not a koala bear!'

The kind blacksmith

Many years ago, in the French town of Auxerre, there lived an old man. He was the priest in the church of St Etienne. Each morning he pushed open the great oak doors of the church and they seemed to get heavier as he got older. One day he felt so old that he just couldn't open them at all. Sadly he sat down on the steps of the church.

The news that the church was shut spread quickly and the people of the town gathered in the sunny square beneath the tall stone spire. 'Whatever is the matter?' they asked. 'Perhaps the doors are jammed.'

Suddenly the crowd parted as a tall, strong man stepped forward. He was the village blacksmith. Standing at the doors he pushed with all his might. The doors creaked and slowly opened wide.

The blacksmith peered into the church as the bright sun streamed through the coloured glass windows. Then he saw the old priest sitting at the foot of the steps.

'Don't worry, Father,' he said in a kind voice. 'I'll come each day to open the doors for you.'

And so he did, and to this day only a strong man can open the doors of the church of St Etienne.

The crafty crocodile

Moumi sat by the side of the great river Nile, which flows through Egypt, shaking goats' milk in a goatskin bag to make butter. It was tiring work and soon her arms began to ache.

Out of the blue-green waters of the Nile a crocodile raised its head and spoke. 'You look tired, little girl. Let me help you churn your butter. I will shake the goat-skin bag in my strong jaws.'

Noumi was pleased to have help with making the butter, but she did not know that the crocodile was a cunning creature. As soon as Noumi held out the bag, he seized it in his strong jaws and swam down the river to a safe place, where he ate up every scrap of the half-made butter.

'Mmmm. Delicious,' he said, smacking his lips.

When Noumi went home and explained what had happened, her mother scolded her for being so silly.

Her father, however, said, 'Never mind, Noumi. I know how to teach that crocodile a lesson. Listen to me.'

Next morning Noumi sat on the bank of the river with

another goatskin bag. She shook it slightly as if she were making butter, but in fact she did not lift it off the ground.

The crocodile raised his head out of the water. 'You look tired, little girl,' he said again. 'Shall I help you to churn the butter?'

'No thank you,' said Noumi. 'Yesterday you stole the butter and ate it up.'

'I'm so sorry,' said the crafty crocodile. 'It was such a long time since I had tasted butter that I couldn't resist it. But this time I really will churn the milk into butter for you to show how sorry I am.'

'Very well,' said Noumi. 'Pick up the bag in your strong jaws.'

The crocodile seized the bag and dragged it into the water, but as he pulled he discovered it was full of heavy stones, not milk. The weight of the stones made the crocodile sink straight to the bottom of the deep river. He had to open his jaws and let go of the bag to come up for air. He was coughing and spluttering.

'Perhaps you won't be in such a hurry to steal things another time,' said Noumi laughing.

The enchanted loch

Cutting deep into the west coast of Scotland is a dark loch with steep, wooded sides. The water there is black and strange. It is said to be enchanted and is called Loch Ness.

Many years ago a small farmhouse stood at the water's edge where a poor farmer lived with his wife and son, who was called Jamie. One evening Jamie's father took his wife in his arms and said kindly, 'I must find work in the town or we will starve. Take care of yourself and the wee lad.' Then he kissed them both goodbye and pushed his small boat out on to the still waters of the loch.

Many months passed and Jamie and his mother feared they would never see his kind face again.

One morning Jamie was collecting firewood from a sheltered beach by the loch when suddenly he heard a squeaking noise at his feet. Looking down he saw a strange creature. It was caught between two stones and its little legs were wriggling helplessly in the air. Jamie laughed and bending down he released the tiny creature which scurried off into the loch.

Jamie watched the circle of ripples disappear across the water. Suddenly it opened up and a great monster towered above him. Jamie was very frightened, but plucking up his courage and looking closer he saw that the beast was just like the tiny creature he had released.

'Thank you for saving my little one,' boomed the monster in a deep voice. 'I am the guardian of the enchanted loch and I can grant you one wish.'

'I wish only for my father's return,' stammered Jamie.

The monster smiled. 'Your father is safe,' he said. 'His boat was smashed to pieces in a storm. Ever since he has lived with me in my kingdom. I am pleased to have found you at last. Now I can return him to his family.'

The monster leant over Jamie and large drops of water fell into the boy's eyes. He blinked and in an instant the monster had disappeared. In his place stood his father holding a large, heavy bag in his hand.

At home he told his delighted wife and son how he had lived in a beautiful palace beneath the loch since his boat had sunk. The monster had given him the bag only this morning. They opened it and found it full of gold. They would never be poor again.

Hanne's storks

The autumn leaves were falling when Hanne saw the storks flying away from their nest on the roof. 'Where are they going?' she asked.

'They spend the winter in Africa,' said her mother, 'but in the spring they'll return to Denmark.'

As the winter snow melted and the first flowers began to show, Hanne looked out for the storks. Every day she searched the sky, but the storks did not come back.

Then one bright sunny morning Hanne looked out of the window. 'They're here!' she shouted.

But the storks flew past to the roof of the bakery. The following day another pair of storks flew over, but they landed on the nest on the schoolhouse. During the next week storks returned to many other houses in the village, and still the nest on Hanne's roof was empty.

'I think they've forgotten the way,' Hanne said sadly. Suddenly she heard a harsh cry. She ran into the garden and saw a pair of storks flying towards the house. They circled round and settled on the nest by the chimney.

Hanne was delighted. 'Our storks have come home at last.'

The fishing trip

Hong Kong harbour is crowded with boats, and Kun-fu's home floats in the harbour too. He lives on a Chinese fishing-junk; a large wooden boat with batwing sails.

'Come!' said his father one evening, 'a school of fish has been sighted! We must prepare for a night of fishing.'

When all was ready, the large sails, which almost blocked out the red sunset, were unfurled. One by one, the junks pulled out; and sailed through the harbour entrance, into the rolling waves of the South China Sea.

When dark, the Chinese fishermen hung bright lanterns on the bows of their junks, to attract fish. Kun-Fu thought they looked like sparkling jewels. They slowly trawled through the night, then, 'Heave in!' shouted his father, and Kun-Fu helped to drag the nets aboard.

They were heavier than usual. Then Kun-Fu saw why. 'Shark!' he cried. 'We have a shark!'

In the nets was a large shark, which fought and turned as it came to the surface. 'Get it!' shouted his father.

But with a leap, the shark splashed back into the sea. Still, it had driven hundreds of fish into their nets.

They had the largest catch, ever.

The carnival dog

The little black dog whimpered, her tail between her legs. Fireworks cracked and sparkled and everywhere the music of the carnival bands filled the streets of the Brazilian city.

Felicia bent to stroke the little dog, who licked her hand in a friendly way. More fireworks exploded in a shower of red and green sparks. The dog whimpered again.

'Have you lost your master?' said Felicia kindly. She picked up the dog and looked at the name tag on its collar. 'Pepita,' she read. There was a telephone number too. 'We'll have to take you home when the carnival is over.'

At that moment a group of dancers in fancy dress came by. They were dancing the samba which they had learned specially for this year's carnival. Felicia joined in, still carrying Pepita, and danced the length of the road. One of the other dancers gave her a garland of paper flowers to wear, which tickled Pepita's nose and made her sneeze.

At the end of the road lay the exotic gardens full of rare jungle trees and plants, and along the paths danced people dressed as jungle animals and brilliantly coloured birds.

Felicia was tired and decided to rest for a while. She sat under a palm tree and watched the musicians and dancers

while Pepita sniffed among the trees, her tail wagging. But when a firework exploded nearby, Pepita ran straight back to the little girl.

It began to grow dark. 'I must go home now,' said Felicia. 'Come along, Pepita.'

At home her father telephoned the number on Pepita's collar.

The little dog's owner, Mr Vasquez, was delighted when he heard that Pepita had been found, and next morning Felicia's father took her to the house overlooking the bay where Mr Vasquez lived.

'Pepita! How glad I am to see you,' exclaimed Mr Vasquez. 'She ran away when the firework display began, and I couldn't find her in the crowd.'

He took Felicia and her father into the garden. There were five black puppies playing on the grass. 'These are Pepita's puppies,' said Mr Vasquez. 'I should like you to have one, if your father agrees.'

He looked at Felicia's father who nodded his head.

'Oh, thank you,' said Felicia and she chose a fat black puppy who looked exactly like Pepita.

Race to Seal Point

'Noisy, uncomfortable things, skidoos,' snorted Jootah's grandfather as Uncle Inoogah switched off the engine of his motor-sled.

'Almost everyone in the Arctic has a skidoo now,' said Jootah.

'I'll keep my dog-team,' said Grandfather. 'A skidoo would shake my old bones to pieces.'

'This is much faster,' said Uncle Inoogah.

'I still think my dog-team would beat you,' replied Grandfather.

'Tomorrow morning then,' said Uncle Inoogah, 'we'll have a race to Seal Point.'

Grandfather agreed. 'You can ride with me, Jootah,' he said. So next morning Jootah helped Grandfather hitch the ten dogs to the sled on their long traces. Uncle Inoogah revved the engine of his skidoo.

'Ready, steady, go!' One of the other Eskimos gave the signal, and they were off. Uncle Inoogah went straight into the lead, but Grandfather's fine team of dogs was not far behind. Then the sound of the skidoo engine stopped.

'Ha! Inoogah's in trouble,' said Grandfather with a grin. As they drew level they saw that the sled pulled by the skidoo had tipped over. 'That's what happens when you go too fast,' said Grandfather.

The dog-team sped on smoothly and silently. After a while they could hear the skidoo coming up behind, and now Grandfather had to stop to straighten out the traces, which had tangled as the dogs changed places during the run. He was still unravelling the long leads when Uncle Inoogah drove past waving happily.

At last Grandfather and Jootah were on their way again, but suddenly, a trace caught on an overhanging piece of ice

and snapped. The dog rolled over on the ice, before getting
up and trotting behind the sled.

'We'll never win with one dog short,' said Jootah.

'We'll see,' said Grandfather. 'Inoogah's stopped again.'
'Engine trouble?' asked Grandfather politely, as the dog
team ran past the silent skidoo.

'I'll soon mend it,' called Uncle Inoogah good-
humouredly. 'You haven't won yet!'

'He'll have to be quick about it,' said Grandfather. 'There
are the huts of Seal Point.'

He cracked his whip over the dogs' heads and as they
began to ride down towards the village, they heard the
engine of the skidoo roar into life again.

The dog-team ran into Seal Point just as Uncle Inoogah
drew alongside in his skidoo.

'It's a draw!' shouted Jootah.

The crossing

Marie lived right at the edge of her country where her father looked after the border crossing. 'Welcome to Luxembourg,' he would call cheerfully, as each car drew up at the great black and white post that barred the road.

One evening, just before Marie's bedtime, her father looked at the big post. 'It's time I repainted this,' he said. 'It looks quite shabby.'

Marie went thoughtfully to bed and the next morning she got up early and ran off to the garden shed.

Later when her father had finished his breakfast, he came out on to the road. His mouth opened in surprise. The great post was now painted in bright colours, with stripes and flowers and stars and diamonds.

'Do you like it, Father?' asked Marie, who had paint all over her face.

Her father laughed out loud. 'Like it?' he roared. 'I think it's terrific.' He bent down close to Marie. 'But I think we'll have to paint it black and white, it's the regulations.' Marie looked sad. 'But maybe we'll do it next week,' he added.

The clever tailor

Once upon a time in Poland there lived a clever tailor. He was a very good tailor and had lots of customers but he got tired of cutting out suits and sewing on buttons all day so he set off to have an adventure. All he carried was his needle and a reel of thread.

He hadn't gone far when he came upon the king's palace. Much to his surprise he saw that rain was pouring down from the sky above the palace although the fields and woods around were bathed in sunshine.

'It is a wicked spell,' the king explained to the tailor. 'I will give my daughter's hand in marriage to anyone who can stop the rain.'

'That's easily done,' said the clever tailor. And he ran up the palace stairs, up and up, until he reached the roof. Standing on top of the very tallest chimney he got out his needle and thread.

'There is a hole in the sky,' he said. 'I will sew it up.' And such was his skill that before you could count to one hundred, he had darned the hole in the sky and the rain had stopped.

So the clever tailor married the king's daughter and lived happily ever after.

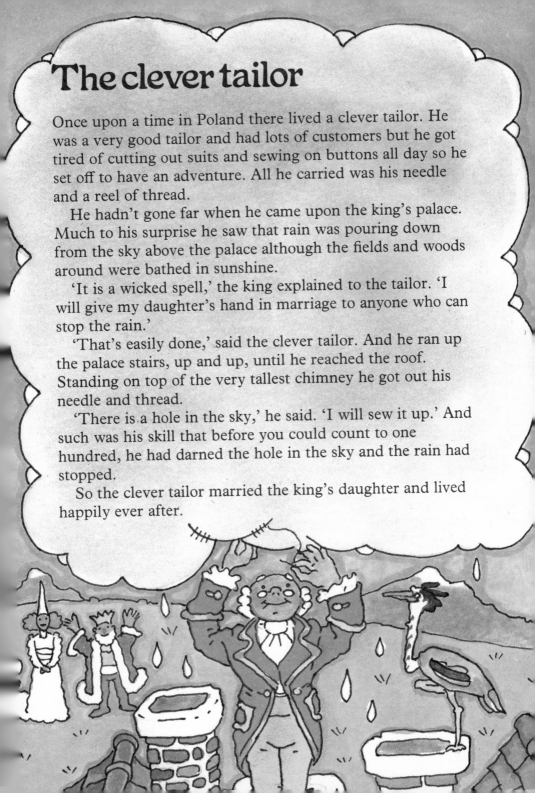

The island

Every October, Bobby and Erica asked to go to 'the island'. They lived in Toronto in Canada and 'the island' was a little island in Lake Ontario.

'Mummy, is it really today we're going?' said Erica one Saturday.

'It certainly is,' said her mother. 'What do you think I'm packing this hamper for?'

'Hurray,' said the two children. Half-an-hour later they were speeding along in their car to the little ferry which would take them to the island. The wind blew gently as they crossed the narrow stretch of water, but the sun shone brilliantly in a cloudless blue sky. Soon the children were jumping off the little ferry on to the rickety island jetty, while their parents followed carrying rugs and picnic baskets.

'We've come at just the right time this year,' said Father. 'The trees are all changing colour.'

Certainly the island was a wonderful sight. Some leaves were dark russet red; some were golden yellow, and others deep, purple-brown. The sky was blue, the sun shone and the air was fresh and clean.

Bobby and Erica scampered ahead of their parents to the

boardwalk which ran along one side of the island. Although
the island was only in a lake, the lake was so huge that it was
almost like being on the seashore, only of course there were
no waves.

The two children found a perfect hollow overlooked by a
little white-painted church. Their father shook out the rugs
while their mother unpacked the picnic hamper. The fresh
air had made them all hungry, so they tucked into
hamburgers and soup, cake and fruit, and coffee and
lemonade. Three fluffy chipmunks, who were not at all shy,
came up for some crumbs and Erica soon had one of them
eating out of her hand.

While their parents dozed, Bobby and Erica chased up
and down the boardwalk and threw pebbles into the
shimmering lake to see who could throw the furthest. Then
they climbed a tree and shook off some of the lovely, golden
leaves.

All too soon it began to get chilly and it was time to catch
the ferry home.

As usual, they had had a lovely time, a last feel of summer
before the long, cold winter settled in.

Snowpaws the tiger

Mehenaz, an Indian princess, was given a white tiger cub for her birthday. Snowpaws walked with her in the palace gardens on a lead of woven gold. He ate the tastiest morsels from the table and at night he slept on silk cushions at the foot of Princess Mehenaz's bed.

But Snowpaws was not completely happy. Through the palace gates he glimpsed the jungle, with its mysterious dark trees and flashing brilliant birds, and he heard the sounds of the jungle animals. At night, as Snowpaws lay awake on his cushions, his sharp ears pricked up when he heard the deep cries of the jungle and he longed to be there.

One day he saw his chance. When Princess Mehenaz put down his lead to pick some flowers, Snowpaws slipped out of the palace gate and ran into the jungle. Startled birds flew up in the air; snakes slithered away, then he heard footsteps.

An old striped tiger stepped out of the undergrowth. 'What are you doing here?' he asked Snowpaws.

'I have come to the jungle where I belong,' said Snowpaws. 'I cannot stay in the palace. I am a tiger.'

'You don't look like a tiger,' said the wise old tiger. 'Show me your sharp claws.'

Snowpaws stretched out gleaming, sharp claws.

'Yes indeed, those are the claws of a tiger,' said the wise old tiger. 'Can you swim in the river as all tigers do?'

Snowpaws jumped into the river and swam to the far bank and back.

'Yes indeed,' said the wise old tiger, 'that is how tigers swim, but can you hunt?'

Snowpaws stole deeper into the jungle, but no matter how swift and silent he was, the other animals saw him coming. His white coat showed up against the dark jungle creepers.

'Alas, Snowpaws,' said the wise old tiger, 'you could never

live in the jungle. You see my stripes. When I stand still no one can see me against the tall grass. My coat is like sun and shadows. Yours is like a bright light. Go back to the palace, little one.'

Snowpaws was sad, although he understood why he could not live in the jungle.

And sometimes on a moonlit night when the sounds of the jungle come through the palace window, he escapes for a while to visit his friend, the wise old tiger.

The Lucia Queen

Ingrid woke before dawn. She was excited because she was to be Lucia Queen on St Lucia's Day in Sweden.

Ingrid's mother helped her into her white dress with the red sash, and placed a crown of whortleberry twigs on her head.

Soon Ingrid heard noises outside her house. Her friends, who were maids of honour, had arrived, each carrying a lighted candle; and the boys were dressed as old men with long beards.

Ingrid picked up the tray of cakes and honey they were going to take to all the houses in the village. Then all the children set off together, singing loudly.

Ingrid and the maids of honour and the old men knocked on the door of every house. They gave out the cakes and carried food to all the animals in the stables and cowsheds. It took a long time to visit each house, because everyone wanted to look at the lights and the costumes.

At last it was time for the Lucia Queen and her procession to go for breakfast in the schoolroom, which was lit with hundreds of candles.

It was a marvellous day; one that Ingrid would remember for the rest of her life.

Oundo the goatherd

Oundo liked looking after the goats. Every morning he drove them out to the scrub land around the African village where he lived.

One very hot day Oundo had to walk a long way before he found a good piece of land for the goats to graze. He sat under a tree and went to sleep in the shade.

He awoke suddenly to hear the goats bleating in alarm. Wild dogs were stalking through the scrub. Oundo seized his stick and rushed forward shouting and beating at the bushes. The dogs turned and ran.

Oundo counted the goats. One was missing – his favourite, Brown Ears.

He followed the trail of the dogs, but there was no sign of Brown Ears.

Oundo searched till it was almost sunset. Then he heard a faint bleat, and another even fainter. He ran to the thorn patch from where the sound came. Brown Ears lay in the thorn patch, and beside her lay two newborn kids.

'Brown Ears, you gave me a fright,' said Oundo. 'I shan't fall asleep again. Now I must take you home.'

He picked up the kids, one under each arm and Brown Ears followed him bleating softly.

77

Louise to the rescue

There are more sheep than people on South Island in New Zealand. East of the snow-peaked mountains are the Canterbury Plains; rich pastures where most of the sheep are reared.

On one of the sheep stations there, Angus the shepherd was listening to instructions from the owner, Mr Oakes. His horse was at his side, his sheepdogs around him.

Mr Oakes was saying, 'I want the flock on the hillside brought down to the grassland for market. It's a big job, I know. Will you be able to manage alone?'

'I'll manage,' said Angus, 'with the help of the dogs.'

At that moment, Mr Oakes' young daughter came galloping up on her pony. 'Hi, Dad!' she cried, 'I've just had my first gallop on Twilight!'

'Now look, Louise,' said her father, 'Don't you go scattering any sheep. Now you have a pony, you ought to be learning to work – not playing around galloping.'

'She could start work with me, if you like,' said Angus.

Mr Oakes stared. 'Could she help?'

'Oh yes, please!' begged Louise excitedly.

'It's a full day's job,' warned her father.

'I'll look after her,' promised Angus.

So it was arranged. Louise felt so proud, setting off with Angus on horseback. The hills rolled in front of them, lit with sunshine.

Once up with the sheep, the dogs began herding them, obeying the whistles from Angus, who shouted instructions to Louise, too. It was very hard work, keeping the sheep together. And then it happened . . . Angus's horse caught its foot in a pot-hole, and fell. Angus was unhurt, but the horse was lame.

'I can't do much without a horse,' he said worriedly.

'I know!' Louise cried. 'I'll fetch you another one!'

'What?' called Angus. 'All the way from the sheep station?' But Louise had gone.

'I'm not playing around galloping, now,' she thought, urging Twilight on.

She reached the stables, and, flinging a halter round one of the horses, led him out.

'Hey!' shouted her father, suddenly seeing her gallop off with another horse.

'It's for Angus!' shouted Louise. 'Don't worry!'

Angus got on to the horse thankfully, and Louise led the lame one behind Twilight. Slowly, they moved the sheep down to the pastures. By evening, a very tired Louise was the hero of the day.

The water giant

Far away in the dark, thick forests of Germany lived two
angry giants who were always quarrelling. Their names were
Trog and Grog.

One day Trog was in his garden planting fir trees, which
he used for matchsticks, when he heard a deep growl behind
him. It was Grog.

'You've planted your trees on my land,' Grog said crossly.

'No I haven't,' answered Trog. 'This is my part of the
forest and I'll plant what I like here, so there!'

They started to push and heave at each other: Trog trying
to push Grog away from his trees and Grog trying to push
Trog off *his* land. They pushed and pushed but they were
both so strong that neither moved at all!

At last Grog got tired of pushing and, dropping to his
knees, began pulling at the ground beneath Trog's feet. 'If I

can't move you, then I'll move the ground instead,' he growled.

'Oh no you don't,' said Trog and he too began to tear at the ground.

They pulled and pulled until suddenly there was a terrible ripping sound and the land split open like an old cloth sack. The tear stretched as far as they could see. It went right across the land to the sea which flooded in filling up the hole completely.

'Now see what you've done, you stupid giants!' Trog and Grog jumped with surprise. Standing behind them was a strange figure dressed entirely in blue. He carried a great staff which was decorated from top to bottom with shells, fishes and beautiful water plants.

'Who are you?' they asked, a little frightened.

'I am the giant of the water places,' he answered in a strong voice. It seemed to flow right over the two sulky giants as they faced each other across the swift flowing river they had made.

'Now you must stay on your own banks. The water is mine and neither of you must ever cross the river again. If you do, I will turn you to stone with my magic.' With these words the water giant turned and slowly melted into the river.

Right up to this day the river Rhine still flows swiftly through the hills of Germany. If you travel there you will find two great rocks facing each other across the waters. So the silly giants must have tried to cross the river after all!

Lee's dragon kite

One day Lee saw a dragon flying towards him. Red, pink and blue it swooped down, lifted again and fell to the ground. Lee picked it up. It was a kite shaped like the old dragons of China.

Lee had often tried to make a kite, but it was too difficult, so he decided to take the kite home.

When his mother saw it she said, 'It's much too big for you, Lee, and it must belong to someone. Your father will ask in the town next market day.'

Lee hadn't realized the kite belonged to someone else and he was very disappointed.

On market day Lee's father came home bringing another man with him. 'This is the kite-maker, Lee. It was his new kite you found.'

'The dragon kite is a special design for the contest in the great city,' said the kite-maker. 'It flew so high and so fast that the cord broke and my kite was lost.'

Lee sadly gave back the dragon kite.

Next market day when Lee's father came home, he was carrying a bundle. 'For you, Lee, from the kite-maker.'

Lee unwrapped the bundle – it was a small dragon kite!

Anni's hat

Anni's mother sat stitching a new hat for the reindeer
round-up that they had every year in northern Finland.
Anni liked the hat. It was made of soft reindeer skin with
many pieces of bright red felt stitched on.

'I'd like blue and white and red beads, too,' said Anni.

Her mother laughed. 'It'll be very colourful.'

Anni was proud of her new hat, and on the first day of the
reindeer round-up she went down to the corral where the
reindeer were being lassoed and taken away by their owners.
Anni looked for her own reindeer which she had been given
for her birthday.

Suddenly everyone scattered as a big reindeer broke loose
from the man who was holding him. Anni ran away quickly,
and her new hat was knocked off in the rush.

'At least you are safe,' said Anni's mother, hugging her
daughter who was almost in tears.

Later, when the last reindeer had left the corral, a man
clapped his hands. 'We have found a hat . . .' he called.

'It's mine,' said Anni excitedly. She pushed through the
crowd and the man put the hat on her head.

'The most beautiful hat at the round-up,' he said.

The balloon trip

'I wish I knew what was eating the young shoots in my vineyard,' grumbled Monsieur Lebon. 'It's a mystery. If this goes on I will make the poorest wine in France.'

Marcel and Danielle had gone to the vineyard to buy wine for Uncle Gaston and Aunt Marie, who were coming to stay. They were looking forward to the visit because Uncle Gaston had promised to take them for a trip in his hot air balloon.

'We'll wave to you if we pass over the vineyard,' they told Monsieur Lebon.

In the evening Uncle Gaston and Aunt Marie arrived with the balloon and its basket in a big truck. Marcel and Danielle couldn't wait to see the balloon, but Uncle Gaston said, 'Be patient. Tomorrow if the weather is fine, we will make the first trip.'

The children hardly slept that night and were up early in the morning. After breakfast they helped Uncle Gaston and Aunt Marie to unload the balloon and basket. They watched as the red and green striped balloon filled with air. At last everything was ready.

'Climb aboard,' called Uncle Gaston. Marcel and Danielle scrambled into the basket, and slowly the balloon lifted into the air. They floated up and up until their house looked like a doll's house. High over the forest they floated, and on the slopes of the hill they could see the vineyard.

'Are we going that way?' asked Marcel.

'We promised to wave to Monsieur Lebon,' said Danielle.

'I think we shall be going right over the vineyard,' said Uncle Gaston.

Far below, the children could see Monsieur Lebon and his sons working among the neat rows of vines. 'Monsieur Lebon!' they shouted. At first he did not see them, then one of his sons caught sight of the red and green balloon and everyone waved. As the balloon reached the edge of the forest, Marcel saw something moving among the vines.

'Can we go lower?' he asked Uncle Gaston, who slowly brought the balloon down a little.

'Over there,' Marcel pointed. 'Can you see?'

'It's a deer,' exclaimed Danielle. 'It must have come from the forest. So that's what has been eating the young vines. Monsieur Lebon will be pleased when we tell him we've solved the mystery.'

Bird's-nest soup

There was once a poor farmer in Java who had a wife and lots of children but hardly any rice to feed them all. One day a friend came along and said, 'Why don't you go to the caves and gather birds' nests instead of slaving over your rice fields? The nests make very good soup and people will pay a lot of money for them.'

The poor farmer thought this sounded a good idea. But before he set off for the caves, he decided to make an offering to his favourite god and pray for good fortune. Although he had only a little food for his wife and children, he gathered up half the rice, coloured it beautiful colours and took it to the temple.

Another farmer, who was much richer, had also decided to take an offering to the temple. But although he left home with a plate full of lovely food, by the time he got to the temple he had eaten it all and there were only a few banana skins and a chicken bone left.

After they had made their offerings the two farmers began to talk and the poor farmer explained that he was going to look for birds' nests. The rich farmer, when he heard the nests could be sold for a lot of money, decided to come too. So the two men set off for the sea caves where the nests were to be found.

The poor farmer went into one cave where he found, not birds' nests, but hundreds of oyster shells, which he gathered up instead, thinking the oysters would make a nice meal for his hungry family.

Meanwhile the rich farmer had gone into another cave, but he was so full of food that he couldn't move, and instead of gathering nests he fell asleep.

Eventually the tide started to rise in the caves and the two farmers had to set off home. When the first farmer got there, he set down his great pile of oysters and started to open them up, and lo and behold, every one contained a beautiful shining pearl, worth far more than any bird's nest.

The other farmer reached home without so much as one bird's nest, only to discover his house burnt down and his fields flooded. When he started to blame his wife she said, 'I only prayed that we should be given a reward as great as your offering in the temple had been.' The rich farmer hung his head in shame.

The king's statue

Long ago, in Persia (which is now called Iran), there lived a king so vain that he ordered a statue of himself to be built, which would be the biggest statue in the world.

'Put it up there, in the hills, where everyone can see it,' he said, 'and decorate it with the finest gold and jewels.'

His people were poor, and needed houses more than statues, but they had to obey. For years they toiled in the hot sun, hacking the stones out of the bare hills, and carving and cutting them.

When the statue was nearly finished, the king arranged a special ceremony. While his people lined the rocky ledges to watch, he himself started to dig out the final stone to finish the statue. But as he pulled the stone from the rock-face, a hidden underground river gushed out of the hole. The people watched as it swept the king away in its flood, never to be seen again.

The tumbling waters crashed against the statue, which began to crumble and sway. Suddenly, it toppled over, and crashed into the flood. The people scrambled and began to gather the gold and jewels washed up on the banks. Now they had finally been rewarded for all their hard work.

Pedro the monkey

Pedro the monkey lived beside a river in the South American jungle. In the river lived an old crocodile who snapped at anyone who tried to cross the river.

One day Pedro said to the crocodile, 'I can cross this river without getting wet and without coming near your big, white teeth.'

'Oh no you can't,' said the crocodile, smiling.

'Meet me here tomorrow, and I'll show you,' said Pedro.

Pedro told his friends that he was going to climb up a tree and along a branch that stuck out over the river. Then he'd jump across to the other side.

But the crocodile, hiding under the river bank, heard Pedro's plan. That night, he slithered ashore, and gnawed halfway through the tree trunk, so that the slightest movement would make it fall.

Next day, Pedro climbed up the tree and along the branch. There was a cracking sound, and the tree swayed. Pedro clung to the branch, as the tree went crashing down.

The tree had fallen right across the river. The crocodile ground his teeth angrily as Pedro laughed and said: 'Thanks, Toothy! Now you've made a tree-bridge across the river, and we can all go over whenever we like!'

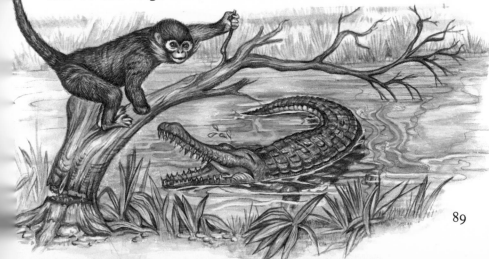

89

Mountain rescue

Paul and his brown dog, Felix, watched the rescue team getting ready to climb the mountain high in the Swiss Alps. Paul's father was in the team which was going to look for a skier who had not returned.

The team put on their warm clothes and climbing boots and fetched their two dogs, Belle and Benni. Belle and Benni were clever dogs. They were usually the first to find people lost in the snow, and they could dig fast with their big strong paws.

Paul played at mountain rescue with Felix. He left Felix at their house at the foot of the mountain. Then he hid behind a pile of snow and shouted for help. Felix bounded straight up to Paul and stood barking and wagging his tail. 'Good boy, Felix,' said Paul.

Next day Paul dug a hole in the snow and hid inside, but Felix soon found him. Paul found better and better places to hide, but no matter how well-hidden he was, Felix always tracked him down. 'Can Felix join your mountain rescue team, Father?' asked Paul.

His father laughed. 'Felix may be good at finding you, Paul, but a mountain rescue dog has to be properly trained.'

One night Paul's father was called to rescue a climber who had fallen on the mountain. Later, an important message came in about another accident, so Paul set out to take the message to the rescue team. It was dark and cold and the snow blew hard into his face. On he struggled into

the biting wind. Suddenly his foot slipped and he fell
heavily, twisting his leg. He could not move and the snow
began to cover him.

When his father and the team came back with the injured
climber, Paul's mother asked anxiously, 'Is Paul with you?'

'We haven't seen him,' replied his father. 'Surely he's not
out on the mountain?'

The rescue team immediately set off again. And this time
Felix went with them. He bounded far ahead of Belle and
Benni, sniffing hard and following Paul's track. Suddenly he
stopped by a mound of snow and started to dig furiously.

'Over here,' shouted Paul's father. 'Felix has found
something.'

The team hurried over and finished digging Paul out. His
father carried him home and he was put to bed. Before he
fell asleep Paul said, 'Felix is a real mountain rescue dog
now, isn't he?'

'He certainly is,' said Father.

Walter Wombat

Have you ever seen a wombat? Wombats are animals that live in Australia and mother wombats carry their babies in a pouch that faces backwards. This is so that when they are busy digging, the earth doesn't spray into the baby wombat's face. The only trouble with this is, mother wombats can't see whether or not their baby is in the pouch.

Listen to what happened to Wendy Wombat one day. She was busy digging a burrow when she realized something was wrong. Her son, Walter, wasn't in her pouch. 'Walter, where are you?' she shouted, but there was no reply. 'Where can he have gone?' she said, puzzled.

So she set off in search of him. First she came to Enid Emu, sitting on her nest. 'Have you seen Walter?' she asked.

Enid looked into the nest. All she could see was eggs. 'He's not here,' she said.

So Wendy went up to Sally Spiny Anteater, who was dipping her long tongue into an ants' nest. 'Have you seen my son?' asked Wendy.

Sally shook her head. She couldn't speak because her tongue was too busy licking up ants.

Wendy, very worried now, looked up a eucalyptus tree.
'Have you seen Walter?' she asked Katherine Koala Bear.
Katherine looked slowly over her shoulder. All she could see
was her own baby, clinging to her back. 'Sorry, he isn't up
here,' said Katherine.

Suddenly, Wendy saw Peggy Platypus. Perhaps Walter
was hiding in her underground nest. But Peggy said that she
was very sorry but no one had been there all morning.

Wendy was at her wits' end. Would she ever see Walter
again? She asked Clive Kookaburra if he had seen him, but
he was too busy laughing to answer.

Then Wendy saw Kate Kangaroo. She hurried over to
her. 'I suppose you haven't seen Walter, have you?' she
asked.

Kate shook her head.

'Are you sure he isn't in your pouch?' asked Wendy in
desperation. They peered inside. And there he was, curled
up round Joey, fast asleep! Wendy was relieved.

'He must have crawled in when I was having a nap,' said
Kate. 'I thought Joey had suddenly put on a lot of weight!'

The Dead Sea

'I've got a surprise for you,' said Ruth's father. 'Today we are going to visit a sea where no one can sink!'

Ruth climbed into the van, and they drove from their home-town of Beersheba all the way to a wide valley of bare rocks. They came down to a big stretch of milky-grey water.

'This is the Dead Sea,' said Ruth's father. 'Now, see if you can sink in that water.'

Ruth waded in. The water felt sticky, and it stung if it splashed on to her mouth or eyes. It tasted very, very salty.

Ruth lay on her back, floating. Her father was right – she couldn't sink. Even if she sat up, as though she was in a chair, she just bobbed about, like a cork.

'You can't sink because of all the salt in the water,' said Ruth's father. 'But because of the salt, nothing can live in the water – that's why it is called the Dead Sea.'

When Ruth got out of the water she found her skin was covered in dry salt, and felt all itchy.

'Now you must have a shower,' said her father. 'After swimming in this sea, you need to wash all over again!'

Beth's Christmas

Many Christmasses ago a little girl called Beth trudged
through the dark, cold, streets of the City of London. It was
snowing heavily and she had been scrubbing steps since the
early morning. Her tiny hands were red and swollen with the
cold. She had earned just two pennies all day long. It wasn't
much towards a happy Christmas.

She passed beneath the great snow-capped walls of the
Tower of London and the icy wind swirled the snow around
her ears. Suddenly, turning a corner, she saw a man step
down from a hansom cab and hurry into a fine house. The
open door cast a warm glow across the snow and Beth saw
that the man had dropped a purse on the pavement.

'Please sir,' she said, her teeth chattering. 'You dropped
this.' And picking up the purse she passed it to him.

The man felt her cold hand and looked very sad. Then he
smiled and opening the purse he gave her a coin. Beth had
no time to thank him before the door was closed.

Alone in the darkness she peered into her hand and saw a
golden guinea. It would be a good Christmas, after all.

Maaui the fisherman

Maaui was such a sickly baby when he was born that his
mother thought he was dead and put his body into the sea.
Fortunately for him, he was found by the Sky God Rangi
who swept him up into the heavens. Rangi grew very fond
of the baby boy and treated him like his own son.

When Maaui was nearly grown up Rangi told him about his family on earth and one day Maaui set off to find them. After much journeying he discovered his mother and his brothers. None of them would believe who he was until he told them how he had been cast into the sea all those years ago and how Rangi had rescued him. Then they welcomed him with open arms and kissed and hugged him.

Maaui's brothers soon got rather tired of him, however, because he was their mother's favourite and she never asked him to do any work.

One day Maaui decided he must show his brothers that he wasn't really lazy so he asked if he could go fishing with them. When they said no, he hid in their canoe, and they didn't discover him until the boat was far out to sea.

The brothers wanted to row back and leave him behind but it was too far to go and, besides, Maaui promised he would find them a good catch. He made them row far further than they'd ever been before and then cast out his own magic fishhook into the sea.

There was a great splashing and a huge fish appeared at the end of Maaui's line, far bigger than any the brothers had seen before. Maaui told them to hold the fish steady and wait while he gave thanks to Rangi for such a splendid catch.

But the brothers got impatient and tried to cut the fish up so they could get it into the boat, which made the giant fish wriggle fiercely about in the water.

And that is why New Zealand is such a mountainous country today, for the big fish which Maaui caught is the North Island, the South Island is the boat they sailed in, and little Stewart Island, at the southern end of New Zealand, is nothing but the anchor of their boat. For Rangi, looking down, saw them all and decided to punish the jealous brothers and, at the same time, to make a new country for his beloved Maaui to live in.

The glass flowers

Tomorrow was Mother's birthday. Anezka had saved
enough money to buy her mother a blue glass vase she had
seen in the village shop. In the mountains in Czechoslovakia
where they lived there were many small workshops where
craftsmen made beautiful glass vases and dishes and figures
to be sold in the shops.

The path down to the village was slippery after the rain
and Anezka's foot twisted on a wet stone. She fell heavily
and the coins she had been holding in her hand rolled away
down the slope.

Scrambling to her feet Anezka ran after them, but she
found only one of the coins lying on the path. The rest had
rolled into the deep moss which covered the mountainside.
Although she searched for a long time, she did not find any
more.

Anezka was dismayed. With only a single coin she could
no longer buy the blue glass vase for her mother.

Slowly she started the long walk home. The sun was
shining and on either side of the path blue, green and gold
lights sparkled. Anezka looked closer. Lying scattered in the
moss were tiny glass beads and glass chippings; they looked
just like a carpet of flowers. They had been dropped from
the crates and baskets of finished glassware, as they were
carried down from the mountain workshops to the village.

Seeing the glass flowers against the dark moss gave Anezka
an idea.

Carefully she gathered the glass beads in her apron and
carried them home. In the shed she spread them out on a
flat piece of wood.

Then she began to arrange them into a picture. Dark
green beads for the moss, blue and gold for the flower petals,
lighter blue for the sky.

It was a slow task and when Anezka had decided where
each piece of glass should be put she carefully stuck it in
place.

As soon as the glue was dry she wrapped the picture in
pretty wrapping paper.

'Happy birthday,' called Anezka next morning, as she ran
into the kitchen with the present.

When her mother opened the parcel she was thrilled with
her special picture of mountain flowers.

'Thank you, Anezka,' she said, hugging her daughter. 'I'm
sure no one else on the whole mountain has such a beautiful
picture as this.'

The talking camel

In a busy market in North Africa, Hasim watched a trader loading up his camels. He heard a voice whispering, 'Help me, please – my master is cruel. He beats me.' It was one of the camels, talking!

Hasim was very surprised, but he wanted to help the camel so he climbed into one of the baskets strapped to its back, squeezed in among the dates inside, and closed the lid.

That night, as they trudged across the desert, Hasim climbed out, untied the camel's rope, and rode quickly away. He rode all night until, at sunrise, he saw a man and some camels just ahead. Too late, he realized it was the trader. They had gone round in a circle!

The trader captured him, and brought him to the local desert chief, to be punished as a thief. But the camel said, 'It is my cruel master you should punish, not Hasim. He tried to save me.'

Everyone was astonished to hear the camel talk – but they realized he spoke the truth. So the chief sent the trader into the desert alone, and gave all his goods to Hasim and his talking camel.

Now Hasim is a wealthy trader, but he is always kind to his camels.

Mr Rajpat's buffalo

Indira sat in the courtyard of her home in India pounding
meal to make chapattis for the family's dinner. It was very
hot and although Indira sat in the shade she soon felt tired.
Thump, thump, thump, went the stick in the bowl, grinding
the fine powder.

'I wish I had an interesting job like Prem,' she thought.
She could see her brother leading the buffalo out to the
fields ready to start ploughing. Prem waved to Indira and
she left her bowl and went to the fence to watch him.

Suddenly Indira heard her mother calling. She turned and
saw that one of Mr Rajpat's buffaloes had broken through
the fence and wandered into their courtyard. 'Oh!' cried
Indira in dismay. 'He's eating the meal.'

Just then Mr Rajpat arrived to catch his buffalo. It was
hard work because the buffalo was enjoying the food so
much. Not until every scrap of meal had been eaten did the
buffalo let Mr Rajpat lead him away.

'Now you will have to grind some more meal,' said
Indira's mother, 'and this time you won't leave it for Mr
Rajpat's buffalo, will you?'

A Danish market

On the Anderssen farm the cock crowed as the sun rose over the gentle countryside. Jørn woke and lay in bed thinking of the exciting day ahead. His brother Niels stretched and yawned and soon both boys were leaping down the stairs for breakfast, for today was market day.

After breakfast, Niels helped his mother pack all the golden brown eggs into the back of the lorry, while Jørn helped his father load up the round, creamy cheeses. Last to go into the lorry were the different sorts of milk – buttermilk, whey, yoghurts and skimmed milk. Then all the family piled in and they set off in the crisp, early morning air to the little town of Bramminge.

Uncle Peder and cousin Orla were waiting for them there. 'Hello everyone,' they called. 'The stall's all ready.' And indeed it was. Its gaily coloured awning flapped in the breeze as they unloaded all the produce. In no time at all the cheeses were laid out on fresh green leaves, the yoghurts lined up in their little pots and the brown eggs heaped in large shallow baskets. Everything did look inviting.

Before long the whole market square was humming with activity and the boys were free to wander around. There were stalls of clothes, secondhand books, fruit, jams and flowers, and even one stall selling nothing but goldfish. Little Niels was very tempted to spend all his money on one, but, as Jørn pointed out, they'd already got a lot of fish in their pond at home.

In the early afternoon, their parents' stall was nearly empty, so the family packed up everything that remained into the lorry, then went over to the old pastryhouse for a big tea of ham and eggs and large helpings of apricot tart and cream. Then after they had said goodbye to Uncle Peder and cousin Orla it was time to go home.

On the way home, Mr Anderssen always stopped the lorry on a little bridge crossing the canal, and the whole family got out to watch the silvery moon come up slowly over the shining water.

'I love market days, don't you, Niels?' said Jørn in bed that night, but a tiny snore was his only reply.

The dancing dolls

Jungko's mother stood the beautiful Empress doll on the top shelf. 'Now everything is ready,' she said.

Jungko was excited because tomorrow was a special day in Japan – the day of the Girls' Festival – and she and her mother had spent many hours making beautiful costumes for the small dolls.

On the top shelf stood the Emperor and Empress, splendid in their richly embroidered clothes. On the next shelf stood the ladies of the court in robes almost as splendid. Below them, the court musicians, each man playing a musical instrument made by Jungko's father.

'Listen,' he said to Jungko, gently plucking the strings of the tiny instruments. 'They really play.'

That night, as Jungko lay on her sleep mat, she dreamed about the figures of the Emperor and the Empress and the court. The musicians were playing and everyone, including Jungko, was dancing. Suddenly she woke up. 'Oh, it was only a dream,' she thought. But then she realized that she could still hear the music. It was coming from the shelves in the living room. Silently Jungko stole in and sat down.

The Emperor bowed low to the Empress. The musicians struck their instruments and the dancing began.

When the dance was over the man who played the lute began to play on his own. His fingers plucked the strings with great skill and the courtiers stood listening. At the end

of the piece everyone clapped and the musicians played
again for the court to dance.

Jungko had no idea how long she sat watching, but at last
the man with the drum beat a sharp rat-tat, rat-tat, and the
dolls went back to their places on the shelves. The note of
the drumbeat changed and Jungko saw that the skin of the
drum had split.

In the morning no one would have guessed that the dolls
had spent the night in music and dancing, unless, like
Jungko, they saw that tiny split in the drum-skin.

The fish dinner

Crafty Arctic Fox loved playing tricks on the animals at the North Pole.

One day he was sitting fishing by a hole in the ice when Polar Bear lumbered up. 'How's the fishing today?' he asked.

'Very good,' said Arctic Fox showing Polar Bear the fish in his basket. 'But I have to go away for a while. If you'd like to take over, you can keep anything you catch.'

Polar Bear agreed. He loved fish. He waited beside the fishing line, dreaming of a fish dinner. The line jerked.

'My first bite!' Polar Bear pulled in the line. On the end was an old bone. Polar Bear threw it back in. The line

jerked again. This time it was a reindeer antler. 'Someone is playing tricks,' thought Polar Bear.

Then he noticed a mound of snow nearby. He peeped over the top and saw Arctic Fox had dug another ice-hole and had pulled out the end of his fishing line. The crafty fox was tying an old Eskimo mitten to the other end of the fishing line.

Polar Bear jumped over the snow mound and growled angrily. Arctic Fox fled, leaving behind his basket of fish. So Polar Bear had his fish dinner after all.

The big race

Maeve patted the gleaming neck of Danny, the chestnut horse that her sister, Bridget, was to ride in the Junior Gold Cup race.

'He's a winner if ever I saw one,' said Jim, the head groom at Clonmar stables in Ireland. 'He jumps like a bird.'

Every day Bridget exercised Danny, while Maeve trotted round on her safe old pony, Bluebell.

Then Bridget caught flu and had to stay in bed. 'Will you take Danny out for me?' she asked Maeve. So Maeve galloped Danny across the green hills and jumped him over the practice fences in the paddock, until she rode him as well as Bridget.

When Bridget was better she came to watch Maeve jumping. 'You are so good,' she said laughing, 'you must ride in the race. I'm out of practice anyway.'

So Bridget rode Danny – and she came first!

'Well done Maeve!' called Jim and Bridget who were watching in the crowd.

'It was Danny really,' said Maeve modestly. All the same she was very proud when she went on to the platform to be presented with the Junior Gold Cup.

The steel band

Winston's big brother was loading his steel drum into a small trailer on the back of his bicycle.

'Can I come and play in the steel band?' asked Winston.

'Perhaps when you're older,' said Joe.

Winston kicked at a stone and wandered off to the river. He sat on the bank trailing a stick in the water. After a few minutes an oil drum came floating downstream. Winston waded a little way into the water. It was quite shallow and with his stick he managed to stop the oil drum and guide it to the bank.

He found a couple of sticks and began to beat the oil drum. It made a good, hollow sound, but nothing like a proper West Indian steel drum.

'What's that racket you're making, Winston?' asked Mr Montgomery who was passing by.

'I'm playing my steel drum,' said Winston.

'I see,' said Mr Montgomery laughing. 'Come to my workshop and we'll see if we can make a real steel drum for you.'

Mr Montgomery cut the oil drum in half. Then he hammered the end into shape, so that he could play different notes on different parts of the drum.

'There's an old pair of drumsticks on the shelf, Winston. You try.'

Winston thanked Mr Montgomery and went off to practise. Every day he went down to the river and practised hard until he could play lots of tunes.

The day of the holiday parade arrived and Joe had to go on his bicycle to the other end of the island. 'I'll be back for the parade at noon,' he promised.

At noon, however, there was no sign of Joe, and the parade was ready to start.

'What shall we do?' said the leader of the steel band.

Winston spoke up. 'I can play instead,' he said. 'I've been practising.'

He ran home to fetch his steel drum. He played a few notes rapidly round the drum.

'That's good,' said the leader. 'Join the band.'

Winston felt very proud as he marched along the road playing with the band. As the parade reached the town square, Joe rode up. 'I'm sorry I missed the parade,' he said. 'My bike had a puncture on the other side of the island and I couldn't get back in time.'

'Well, thanks to Winston, everything was fine,' said the leader of the band. 'Next time you must both play.'

Sheep rescue

It was spring in the Welsh hills, and Ivor the shepherd was rounding up the sheep and bringing them down to the valley to be sheared for the summer.

'Hup, hup, hup,' he called to Taff his sheepdog. 'Ho, ho, jiff, jiff, jiff, jiff.' It sounded like nonsense to anyone else but Taff understood, and did exactly what he was told.

When Ivor spotted a sheep he sent Taff round behind it, slowly, slowly, and Taff got close without scaring the sheep and making it run off. Then he would bring the sheep down to join the rest of the flock. By dinnertime most of the flock were gathered together, and Ivor and Taff drove them down the valley to the farm.

This was the bit Taff liked best. He ran from side to side behind the flock, moving them towards the pen. Once one sheep was in, the rest soon followed.

Ivor had just closed the gate when Owen, the farmer's son, came running up. 'Ivor, Ivor, I've seen a sheep trapped on a ledge – up on the cliff on the big mountain, come quickly!'

'Right,' said Ivor, 'I'll come straightaway.' Off they went up the hillside, with Taff at their heels. Up, up went the

path, getting steeper and steeper, and they had to be very careful not to slip. At last they reached the foot of the cliff, and there, halfway up, they saw the poor sheep, bleating sadly.

'Good boy Owen,' said Ivor. 'She looks like one of ours. You stay here, I'll soon have her down.'

The cliff was steep, but Ivor had been rescuing sheep for years, and he quickly climbed up to the ledge where the sheep was stuck. As he climbed he talked softly to the sheep so it would not be frightened and jump off.

He edged towards the sheep, grabbed it, put it round his neck and held it firmly with one hand. Then he climbed back down again with the sheep around his neck. Owen was sure he would fall, but Ivor knew what he was doing and they were soon safe at the foot of the cliff.

Then it was over to Taff, who coaxed the frightened sheep back down the valley to the farm. Owen and Ivor followed – hungry, thirsty and tired, but pleased with their day's work.

An underwater world

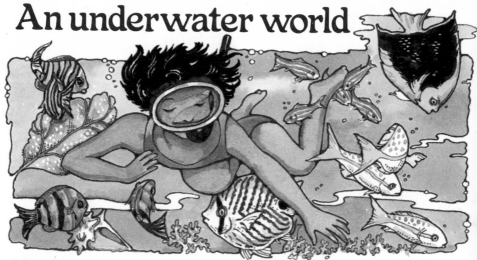

Living in the Seychelles Islands, Sadie learned to swim very young, but she was still a bit frightened of the water.

For her sixth birthday, her mother gave her a snorkel-mask, which lets you see underwater. They went down to the coral beach, and Sadie's mother fixed the mask on for her. They both swam along, and when Sadie put her face down into the water, she saw an amazing world.

The coral looked like coloured rocks carved in strange shapes. Long strands of seaweed waved to and fro, as though they were doing a slow, dreamy dance. And what fishes Sadie saw! There were slithery ones, like snakes; cheeky-looking little red ones, darting about; a fat one that opened and closed its big mouth, as if it was singing; and a flat fish with yellow and blue stripes like a football shirt.

Sadie swam slowly on the surface, gazing down at all these wonders. Then she realized suddenly that she had been swimming out of her depth for a long time, and it hadn't frightened her at all.

She looked up and saw her mother, swimming nearby. 'This is a wonderful mask,' said Sadie, 'and a wonderful birthday!'

Turkish delight

Sultan Selim, ruler of Turkey, was worried. 'What can I give my wife for her birthday?' he asked the Grand Vizier Nedim. 'She has everything already.'

Nedim thought, then said, 'Why not ask your chef Yusuf to create a special dish for the Sultana?'

'An excellent idea. See to it right away,' said Selim.

Nedim hurried to tell the chef, pleased with his clever idea, but Yusuf was terrified. 'What can I do?' he asked Ashik the kitchen boy. 'I can't think of anything new to make.'

As the Sultana's birthday approached, Yusuf became more upset. Ashik felt sorry for him. 'Sir,' he said, 'may I try?'

'Anything,' said Yusuf.

So Ashik began to mix ingredients in a bowl. A sprinkle of this, a touch of that, a drop of something else. Finally, he produced a pink, jelly-like mixture which he cut into squares and dusted with fine sugar. 'Taste one,' he said.

Yusuf tasted. 'Delicious,' he said. 'Clever, clever boy.'

The rosy sweets were placed on a golden dish and given to Nedim who gave them to Selim who gave them to his wife and to this day the sweets are called Turkish delight.

The blue boy

Long ago in the city of Venice in Italy lived a small boy
called Bruno. He was very poor and helped his father on the
canals with his old gondola.

One day Bruno was sitting by the landing stage, dangling
his feet in the water, when a very fine gondola glided into
sight. The gondolier had fine silk breeches and an
embroidered jacket and on his head he wore a wide-brimmed
hat. As the shiny black and gold boat drew closer, Bruno
saw a small, fat boy sitting on a pile of satin cushions. He
was dressed entirely in blue silk except for a white lace ruff
around his neck. He looked very sulky.

The boy caught sight of Bruno's ragged figure and,
standing up to see better, he started to laugh. Bruno felt
ashamed, but as he turned to walk away he heard a loud
splash. The blue boy had laughed so much that he had
fallen out of the gondola. The smart gondolier was so
surprised he dropped his oar and watched helplessly as the
boat drifted away.

Bruno couldn't help laughing but he ran down the steps
and pulled the little, fat boy from the water by the seat of

his trousers. What a sight he was. His fine clothes were covered in mud and his ruff was around his ears.

'Well, we don't look so different, after all,' said Bruno.

'I'm sorry,' whimpered the blue boy, standing there dripping wet. 'I'll never laugh at anyone's ragged clothes again.' He wiped a bit of mud from the end of his nose.

Bruno took him into the house where his mother dried the boy's wet clothes in front of the stove. When the blue boy was about to leave he turned to Bruno and said, 'Thank you for saving me, my father will reward you for your kindness.'

The next day the same fine gondola glided up to Bruno's landing stage. Inside was the blue boy and his father, a wealthy merchant of Venice. They had a new warm set of clothes for Bruno – and, best of all, a beautiful new gondola for Bruno's father.

'You have my thanks indeed,' said the rich merchant. 'And,' he leant close to Bruno's ear, 'I think all that mud has taught my son a lesson. I hope he will never laugh at anyone again!'

The ugly animal

There was an animal that lived in the Kruger National Park who was very unhappy. For all the other animals said that he was the ugliest animal in South Africa. 'Just take a look at yourself,' said Jackal. 'Then you'll see what we mean.'

So he took a look at his reflection in the water-hole. And he did see what they meant. He had a funny, nobbly face and stumpy, curved tusks. He had small eyes and a rough, wrinkled skin. Coarse hair stuck up here and there along his back. He had a thin tail that stuck bolt upright when he ran.

Have you guessed what animal he is? Yes, you're right! He's a wart-hog!

Poor Wart-Hog. Everywhere he went, animals would make fun of him. 'Call those funny little things tusks?' said Elephant, raising his head to show off his own beautiful

tusks. 'Why, tusks should curve outwards, like mine, not inwards towards your face like yours.'

'Call that ugly hair a mane?' said Lion, proudly tossing his locks. 'Why, a mane should be long and golden and flowing like mine, not just a few horrible straggly hairs like yours.'

Wart-Hog grew more and more unhappy. Everyone laughed at him, and so he strayed further and further from the other animals. He was lonely but at least he wasn't reminded of how ugly he was. When he drank at a water-hole he kept his eyes tight shut so that he wouldn't see his reflection.

One evening he went to his water-hole and started to drink. Even though his eyes were tight shut, a tear still managed to squeeze out. And then he heard a kind voice at his side say, 'Why are you crying, Wart-Hog?'

'Because I'm the ugliest animal in South Africa,' he said.

'*I* don't think you're ugly,' said the kind voice. 'I think you're the handsomest wart-hog I've ever seen,' and he felt a friendly shoulder brush against his.

Wart-Hog opened his eyes and looked round in surprise. Who on earth could have said such a thing? There, standing very close beside him, was a beautiful lady wart-hog! They fell in love and spent the rest of their lives together. And, if ever an animal called Wart-Hog ugly, he'd smile at his lovely lady wart-hog and then reply, 'I may be ugly to *you*, but to other wart-hogs I am very handsome.'

The lonely budgie

In Australia, budgerigars are wild and fly about in great flocks. There was one budgie called Barry who was smaller than the rest of his flock, and he found it very hard to keep up. 'Wait for me,' he'd cry, but they never did.

One day, the thing that Barry dreaded would happen, did. He was left behind. He flew about looking for them. But it was no use. Barry made a little hole in the ground and sat in it. How lonely he felt.

In the morning he flew in search of a friend. After several hours he came to a sheep station. 'Sheep wouldn't make very good friends,' he thought to himself. Then he saw Susan, a little girl, playing in the garden. She looks friendly, he thought and flew down on the grass beside her. Now Susan was lonely too, and was delighted to see Barry.

Barry's new home was a large cage. He could watch television and hear all the conversations going on. And every day Susan let him out of his cage so that he could fly round and get some exercise.

Barry never felt lonely again. And he was far happier living with Susan than he'd ever been trying to keep up with the other budgerigars.

Birthday surprise

Inger and Birgitta lived in a neat white house overlooking the town of Stockholm in Sweden. The two girls were twins and were as alike as two peas in a pod. Each one had long blonde hair tied in plaits with a bright red ribbon. Each wore a pretty white blouse with a blue skirt, and each wore snow white socks.

One day they were sitting in front of their house looking across the town towards the sea. They looked very thoughtful and then all of a sudden they both spoke at once.

'What is going to happen?' they asked. They were so alike they often said the same thing.

'You mean about our birthday party?' asked Inger.

'Yes,' replied Birgitta. 'Do you think they've forgotten? It is tomorrow, after all.' She looked very serious.

The next day was their birthday and after school they came sadly home. No one had said anything all day and they had no presents at all.

'Happy birthday!' There, in front of them, was a table laden with party food and presents and all their friends were there.

The twins laughed. 'Gosh, what a surprise,' they said, both together of course.

Tomi the woodpecker

Suma lived in an American Indian village, near a forest. Her father was a wood-carver, and he was making a wooden statue of a giant eagle, to stand on top of the archway at the entrance to the village. There was going to be a special ceremony on Saturday, when the eagle would be put in place.

Suma went down to the forest clearing to watch her father carving the eagle out of a big tree-trunk. Then she wandered away into the trees, to find her friend, Tomi the woodpecker.

Tomi thought the statue on the archway should be of a woodpecker, not an eagle. 'Woodpeckers are much more clever,' he said. 'They can peck holes in wood; eagles can't.'

Just then, Suma heard a cry. She ran back to the clearing, and found her father had cut his hand. They went home, and Suma's mother bandaged the cut. Her father was very

upset, because now he couldn't hold his carving tools
properly, and wouldn't be able to finish the eagle in time.

Suma had an idea. She went off into the forest and found
Tomi. 'Please help us, Tomi,' she said. 'You could finish the
carving with your sharp beak.'

'Well, I'm not a wood-carver,' said Tomi, 'but I'll try.'
And he set to work, tap-tap-tap, tap-tap-tap, pecking away
at the wood. When Suma went home that evening, Tomi
was still tapping away. And as she fell asleep, she was sure
she could hear, far off in the forest, the sound of tap-tap-tap,
tap-tap-tap. . . .

In the morning, she hurried to the clearing. Tomi was
sitting on the branch of a tree, fast asleep – and there was
the statue of the eagle, all finished!

'Oh, thank you, Tomi, thank you!' she cried.

Tomi woke up. 'It was a pleasure,' he said, and went to
sleep again.

Suma rushed home and fetched her father. He stared at
the finished statue in amazement. 'It's beautiful,' he said,
'but who did it?'

'Tomi, the woodpecker,' said Suma, pointing to the
branch. Tomi flapped his wings and bowed.

'Thank you so much, Tomi,' said Suma's father. 'Now
we can have the ceremony after all. And as soon as my hand
is better, I'll start making the most splendid carving of a
woodpecker!'

Sir Tom

'Tom Thumb! Tom Thumb!' called the children as they
ran around the school playground.

Tom was very small, but he didn't like being teased by the
others. He wished he could suddenly grow a few centimetres.
Then no one could call him Tom Thumb again.

The bell rang and everyone hurried back into school.
Miss Green's lessons were always interesting and today she
was talking about knights and castles in England long ago.
'I've got something exciting to tell you,' she said. 'Next week
I am taking you on a trip to look round a castle. Then you
will be able to see for yourselves the things we have been
talking about this morning.'

It was a long drive to the castle, but at last the children
tumbled out of the coach and followed Miss Green across
the drawbridge and through the great stone entrance.

There was so much to see. They climbed a narrow,
winding staircase to look out from the top of the tower.
They shivered in the cold, dark dungeons and they looked
down a deep well covered by an iron grating. 'Be careful you
don't slip down through a hole in the grating, Tom,'
laughed the children. 'You're small enough.'

At lunchtime the class picnicked on the bank of the moat
and threw crumbs to the swans.

'Before we go home,' said Miss Green, 'we must look at
the room where the armour and weapons are kept.'

The children thought this last room was the most exciting.
There were huge swords and shields, axes and lances, and
suits of shiny armour.

The guide showed them the different weapons. Finally he

said, 'And this is a suit of armour made for a child. Would one of you like to try it on?'

Everyone put up their hand, but the guide said, 'It'll have to be someone who isn't too big. How about you?' He pointed to Tom.

'Me? Yes, please,' said Tom. He stood in front of the class while the man helped him to buckle on the armour and when he tried to walk he squeaked and clanked horribly.

'Now you can see it properly,' said Miss Green. 'What a good thing Tom was here. No one else was the right size.'

Tom waved the small sword around his head.

'Sir Tom,' said the guide, which made everyone laugh. And from then on Tom was always known as Sir Tom, and he didn't mind that at all.

The big blue fish

Many of the people who live on the Pacific islands travel from island to island on little boats called outriggers.

Meheui was a small boy who lived on one of the Solomon Islands. One day his father allowed him to borrow his outrigger to visit his grandmother, who lived on a nearby island.

He had no trouble getting there but, on his return journey, he hit a bad storm. Soon the waves were dashing Meheui and the outrigger against the coral reef and Meheui was very frightened.

Suddenly, everything went black. When Meheui opened his eyes he was underwater, and a big blue fish seemed to be leading him to safety through the silent and beautiful world of pink coral.

The next thing he knew he was lying on the seashore, gasping for breath, his father leaning over him. The outrigger was safe beside him.

After that Meheui often thought about that beautiful underwater world he had visited and the big blue fish who had led him to safety. He sometimes looked out for it when he went fishing with his father, but he never saw it again.

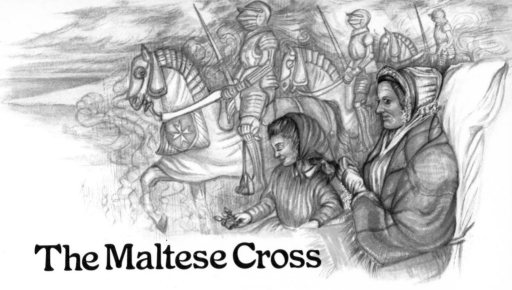

The Maltese Cross

Rosa leaned on the wooden balcony and sighed. Below her stretched the beautiful island of Malta, with a strip of blue sea beyond. It was a very pretty view but Rosa was bored. She had been ill and could not go to school.

In the garden below she saw her granny making lace in the sunshine. She ran down to her. 'I'm bored!' she said.

Granny's black eyes twinkled. 'You must be feeling better!' she said.

Rosa asked, 'What is the pattern on the lace?'

'It is our Maltese Cross, the emblem of the Knights of St John,' Granny explained.

'Did we really have Knights here?' Rosa asked.

Granny nodded. 'Long ago,' she said, 'Malta was ruled by these Knights, who did much good.'

The lace bobbins danced in her busy fingers.

She went on, 'They built massive forts and churches, and our capital city, Valletta, too.'

'Where are they now?' asked Rosa drowsily.

'Napoleon drove them away. But did you know they return each year from other lands, for the feast of St John?'

But Rosa was asleep, dreaming about Knights in shining silver, all wearing the Maltese Cross.

The lost shield

Mutara heard the cry for help again. It was a strange, thin cry and it came from the pit dug by the hunters of his tribe in central Africa.

He peered over the edge of the pit and in the bottom he could just make out the green and gold zigzag pattern of a snake. Mutara had been warned by his father to keep away from snakes, for many were poisonous.

'Let me out,' said the snake. 'I won't harm you.'

Mutara shook his head.

'Let me out,' said the snake again. 'I am of no use to your hunters. They cannot eat me.'

'How do I know you won't bite me if I help you?' asked Mutara.

'You have my word as King of the Snakes,' replied the snake. 'I would not repay your kindness by hurting you.'

Mutara hesitated.

'If you help me out of this pit,' the snake went on, 'I will

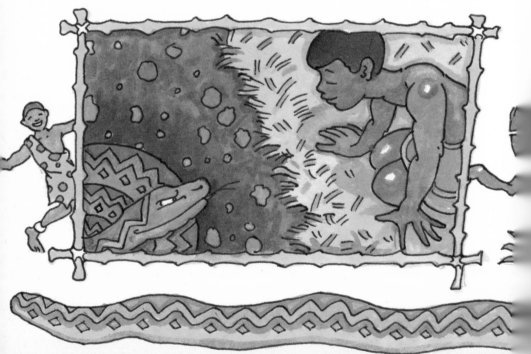

show you where to find the lost shield of Katangesi.'

Mutara was astonished. The shield of Katangesi had belonged to a great chief long ago, and it was his tribe's greatest treasure. But when Mutara was a baby another tribe had stolen it by a trick.

'Is this true?' asked Mutara. 'Do you really know where the shield of Katangesi is hidden?'

'Indeed,' replied the King of the Snakes, 'for did not the thieves set snakes to guard the hiding-place? But a word from me and they will let you take back the shield.'

Still feeling a little frightened Mutara swung down the rope hanging at the side of the pit, lifted the snake on to his shoulders and climbed back up the rope.

The King of the Snakes slithered away through the trees with Mutara following close behind. For a day and a night they journeyed and came to a cave in the hills, guarded by snakes, just as the King had said.

He gave a command and the snakes guarding the cave slid away. Mutara stepped inside. There on a rock lay the shield of Katangesi.

'Our tribe will always be grateful to you,' Mutara said to the King of the Snakes. And when he returned to his tribe there was great feasting and rejoicing for the return of the lost shield of Katangesi.

The watchful eagle

High up in the mountains of Switzerland, where the air is
like ice, there lived a girl called Helga. The winter was her
favourite time of year because there was soft, white snow all
around her house.

One morning she was walking high on the snow-covered
hills when she tripped in a deep drift and tumbled over and
over down a steep slope. She was about to plunge over the
edge of a cliff when suddenly she felt herself floating into the
air. Great wings beat over her head and then she was lifted
gently down to the small garden of her house. It was a great
eagle who had saved her.

'Take care, little one,' he said. 'I am the guardian of
mountain children, but you ought to look where you're going.'

Helga thanked him warmly and kissed him on the end of
his beak. The eagle blushed and ruffled his feathers. Then
he gave a great beat of his wings and soared high over the
mountain tops.

If you ever travel through the Swiss mountains, keep a
sharp look out. You may just catch a glimpse of the guardian
of children soaring in the high, blue sky.

Singapore tri-shaw

To the south of Asia is the island of Singapore, with its busy narrow streets and shops covered with bright decorations.

Lien was cycling home from school; weaving his way through the back-streets where washing stretched across on long poles.

His father looked gloomy. 'The rickshaw has broken,' he said sadly.

Lien was troubled. How could money be earned if his father couldn't work? 'I will mend it,' said Lien.

His father sighed. 'I wish you were strong enough to help me pull people, too,' he said, and went to rest. The rickshaw was very old but they were too poor to buy a new one.

Lien wondered if a wheel from his bicycle would do to mend the rickshaw. He put it against the rickshaw to see. Then, he had a marvellous idea. . . .

Much later, he fetched his father, who stared in amazement. For Lien had fastened his bicycle to the front of the rickshaw, so people could be pedalled along!

'No more pulling for you!' cried Lien, 'and I can use it, too. I shall call it a tri-shaw!'

Clever Ki-ki

In the green rain-forests of South America, the vast Amazon river gleams through the steamy jungle.

Mayta, a native girl, lived in a thatched village by the river. She was well-known by all the tribe, for she had a blue and yellow macaw, named Ki-ki. Mayta had found the macaw while walking in the forest. Ki-ki was a baby bird and lost, so Mayta looked after him, and now the bird would not leave her side.

'I shall teach him to talk!' Mayta told her friends.

'Talk!' scoffed one boy, called Capac. 'I would rather have it cooked for dinner!'

Mayta walked away crossly and gave Ki-ki some nuts, his favourite food. 'Here's a nut,' Mayta would say, and Ki-ki could crack open even the hardest nut with his beak.

So it wasn't surprising that when Ki-ki started to speak, the only thing he would say, was 'Here's a nut!'

But Capac didn't laugh. He was jealous of the way Ki-ki followed Mayta everywhere. 'Stupid thing!' he scowled, and determined to catch the macaw.

But one day, when all the children had been playing in the jungle, Capac did not come back with them.

'Where can he be?' asked Mayta, worried. 'Soon it will be dusk.' No one should be alone in the jungle at dusk. For then, the wild-cats and jaguars prowl. They waited, but Capac did not come.

'We must go back and look for him,' said Mayta. So they set off, into the jade-green twilight.

'Go find Capac!' Mayta ordered Ki-ki. The macaw squawked and flew on ahead.

'Capac!' the children shouted, but there was no answer. Suddenly Ki-ki started to screech loudly and they ran towards the noise.

'Capac!' called Mayta.

'Here!' came back a voice, mixed with Ki-ki's screeches.

They found him, lying on the ground with a sprained ankle.

'I'm glad to see you,' he gasped, thankfully. 'It will soon be dark.'

'We must hurry,' said Mayta. 'Thank goodness Ki-ki found you so quickly,' and the others agreed.

Capac hung his head. 'I'm sorry I was nasty about him,' he said. 'From now on, I promise I'll be his friend.'

Mayta was pleased. So was Ki-ki. He squawked and flew around, then landed on Capac's head.

'Here's a nut!' he screeched, 'Here's a nut!'

And everyone laughed.

The angry teacher

At the edge of a small Dutch village, amongst a clump of tall poplar trees, stood a tiny white schoolhouse.

One morning, as the children of the village entered the schoolroom, they found a new schoolmaster waiting for them. He looked very grumpy and was so tall and thin he nearly touched the ceiling. All day long he snapped and shouted and was cross with everyone. The children longed for the bell to ring so that they could go home. At last the hour arrived and the boy who sat right at the back of the class, whose name was Jan, reached up and took hold of the bell rope.

'How dare you ring the bell without asking,' snapped the angry master. 'Never, never touch that bell rope again, do you hear.' Springing down the room like an angry beanstalk he opened the door and scowling back at the children he added, 'Go home, all of you, now!' They all ran out as quickly as they could.

The following Sunday the schoolhouse bell started to ring in a very strange way. Sometimes it was fast, then slow, then it would pause and then it would start again. When Jan heard the bell he ran from the fields to see what was wrong. When he reached the schoolroom he was very surprised. There, his long arms and legs tangled in the bell rope, was his new schoolmaster. As he struggled to free himself he bounced up and down and all the time the bell clanged.

'Get me down,' he squeaked, as he caught sight of Jan.

Jan stood still for a moment, then he said, 'But Sir, you told me never to touch the bell rope again.'

'I'm sorry,' said the master, swinging against the wall with a bang. 'I promise I won't be cross again, only please help me down.' He bounced off the floor and sailed into the air again.

Jan grabbed the end of the flailing rope and very soon the poor man was untied. He fell to the ground like a bag of sticks. 'Thank you,' he said in the quietest voice Jan had ever heard.

From that day on he was never cross with the children again, but he never went near the bell rope. It was Jan who rang the bell when it was time to leave.

Meera stops a thief

Meera the cow lived in Delhi. But she wasn't an ordinary cow – she was a *sacred* one, which meant that she could go where she pleased without anyone stopping her. She never had to learn the road-safety rules, because whenever she wanted to cross the road, all the traffic would stop for her.

Meera was very happy but sometimes she wished she could be of more use to the people of Delhi.

One day, as Meera was walking through the street market she saw a man steal a knife from a poor woman's stall.

'Stop, thief,' shouted the woman, but it was no use. The man had leapt on to his motorcycle and was roaring away.

This was Meera's chance. Quickly, she walked across the narrow street and lay down, completely blocking the way. The thief beeped his horn and shouted but Meera wouldn't budge.

A crowd of people surrounded the thief and the woman was given back her knife. She looked round for Meera in order to thank her, but, in all the commotion, Meera had slipped away, a big smile on her face. She had done something useful at last.

Thanksgiving dinner

'Morning, Mrs Jackson,' said Billy to the old lady feeding corn to her turkey.

'Are you looking forward to Thanksgiving, Billy?' she replied.

'Yes, my grandma is coming home to America specially to spend Thanksgiving with us. We're having turkey and cranberry sauce and lots of good things.'

'That'll be nice,' said Mrs Jackson. 'I raised this turkey for my Thanksgiving dinner, but he's much too big for me to eat on my own. Besides I've become fond of him, keeping him in my backyard. I call him George.'

When he got home Billy told his mother: 'Mrs Jackson hasn't any family, and she can't eat George for her dinner, so do you think she could spend Thanksgiving with us?'

'Of course,' said his mother. 'What a good idea.'

So Mrs Jackson didn't spend Thanksgiving on her own after all. Everyone had a delicious dinner; Mrs Jackson and Billy's grandma talked together about the old days; and George stood gobbling in the backyard waiting for his next handful of corn.

The goose-girl

Lady Frederika called to the goose-girl and whispered in her ear. 'No, my lady, I dare not,' replied Klara.

'Only for a day. I'm tired of walking in the castle garden. Nothing exciting ever happens,' said Frederika.

So Klara and Frederika changed clothes and Frederika drove the geese into the great Black Forest in Germany.

'Be quiet,' said Frederika to the hissing birds, 'or a wolf will come and eat you up.'

The geese flapped their wings and ran deeper into the forest. Frederika followed, running clumsily in Klara's heavy wooden shoes. Low branches whipped her face and scratched her hands. Finally she tripped over a stone and fell into a patch of mud.

Then she heard a low growl. Two eyes glared at her from among the trees; and out stepped a wolf.

'Good morning, goose-girl,' said the wolf. 'I see you've lost your geese. I was hoping for a fat goose for my dinner, but now I shall have to eat you up instead.'

'You can't eat me,' said Frederika. 'I am the baron's daughter. He will send his hunters to catch you.'

'If you are the baron's daughter,' said the wolf, 'show me your fine clothes.'

136

Frederika looked down at her skirt. It was old and patched and spattered with mud. 'I am the baron's daughter,' she insisted, 'and I live in the castle.'

'If you are the baron's daughter, where are your fine shoes?' laughed the wolf.

Frederika looked down at the heavy wooden shoes. 'I changed places with the goose-girl. She is walking in the castle garden wearing my fine clothes and my satin shoes.'

'Very clever, goose-girl,' snarled the wolf, who didn't believe a word. 'But if you are the baron's daughter, show me your fine hands.'

Frederika held out her hands. They were scratched and red and covered in mud.

'You're not the baron's daughter.' The wolf showed his teeth. 'You're the goose-girl and I'm going to eat you up.'

Just then the shrill notes of a hunting horn rang out. The wolf heard the horn and fled into the forest. Frederika ran towards the hunters who took her back to the castle.

The baron was angry when he heard what Frederika had done, but happy to see her home safely.

'I will never go out of the castle garden again, Father,' promised Frederika. 'Today was a bit too exciting for me.'

Ganba the serpent

Long ago, in the dreamtime of Australia, there were many of the people called Aborigines living in that land. But none of them dared to live in the great treeless plain called Nullarbor. For Nullarbor was the home of a mighty, magic serpent called Ganba who ate people. Although the Aborigines might hunt kangaroos or emus for half a day's walk into the plain, they always returned to their camps at night.

Now it happened once that Ganba the serpent came out from the Nullarbor Plain into the land where the Milbarli tribe lived. And he sat down to rest by Wandunya Lake where the people of the Milbarli tribe, and also many animals, went to get water.

Ngabbula, the spike-backed lizard, saw Ganba and ran to warn the Milbarli people, for they often helped him by throwing him the scraps from their meat.

So the tribe could not fetch any water. They waited long for Ganba to leave, but he did not go. The babies cried until they had become so weak from lack of water they could scarcely murmur. Then Milbarli, the leader of his tribe, spoke to the two best hunters. They were Meeda, whose name means 'small iguana', and Yoong-ga. And all three

agreed that they would try to kill Ganba so that the tribe
could drink.

The three men took their spears and crept up behind the
serpent. They threw the spears and each one pierced the
serpent's heart, but he did not die. For hours they fought
until at last Ganba began to weaken and he tried to hide in
the sand around Wandunya Water. So Milbarli pulled him
and Meeda hit him and Yoong-ga pushed him, and all the
men and women of the tribe came and helped the three men.
At last the magic in Ganba was beaten and he turned into
stone, and he is there still by Wandunya Water.

Milbarli and Yoong-ga made a dance and songs about the
great battle. These were passed down through the tribe to
their children and their children's children. Long after, the
people of that area still danced the Beeja-Beeja-Ma dance to
show how their dreamtime brothers and sisters killed Ganba
the serpent.

Port-of-Spain

Many years ago Connie's father was a shop-keeper in
Port-of-Spain in Trinidad. Her family had lived in
Port-of-Spain since her great-great-great grandfather had
been brought over from Africa as a slave.

Connie loved helping in the shop, measuring cottons and
silks for crinolines and selling bonnets and parasols. But best
of all she liked going with her parents to the harbour each
month when tall ships arrived from Europe.

She sat in their little cart and looked after Sugar the pony,
while her parents went in search of the goods they had
ordered.

Sailors staggered past with bales of shimmering silks and
satins, crates of glass and china, boxes of books and
iron-bound chests, which she was sure were full of
diamonds and rubies. Once she saw a huge piano being
carefully lowered on to the quay.

On the way home, her father always gave her a little
present 'for looking after Sugar'. It was always a present
from Europe. No wonder Connie loved visiting the harbour!

The grateful mermaid

Gunnar and his father, Knut, were fishermen. One morning they were sailing back to their home at the end of a deep fiord on the coast of Norway.

Gunnar was sitting in the bow when he heard a small voice. 'Please, will you set me free?' it said. Gunnar turned and was surprised to see a beautiful little mermaid caught in the nets piled on the deck.

Gently he lifted her free. She was so tiny that she was no longer than his hand. She flicked her tail and opened her deep blue eyes. 'Thank you,' she said, smiling shyly at him. 'You are very kind and I will not forget. I will watch over your boat from now on whenever you visit my kingdom of the sea.'

Gunnar placed her carefully in the water and watched her swim away.

'Are you dreaming again, son?' It was Knut.

Gunnar blinked. He looked at the still waters. There was no sign of the mermaid. Had he been dreaming after all?

The rose-red slippers

In the last days of ancient Egypt, when Amasis was Pharaoh,
it was feared that the Persians would invade Egypt, for they
were conquering all the known world. So, to add to Egypt's
strength, the Pharaoh welcomed many Greeks to settle in his
country. He gave them the city of Naucratis, near the mouth
of the Nile, to be their own.

In Naucratis, there lived a wealthy merchant named
Charaxos. One day, as he strolled through the market place,
he saw that a beautiful Greek girl was being sold in the slave
market. Charaxos so pitied the girl that he decided he would
buy her. The girl's name was Rhodopis and she had been
captured from her home by pirates who had sold her into
slavery. Charaxos was so enchanted by Rhodopis' beauty
that he gave her a house built round a secret garden, and
servants to attend her. He showered her with rich gifts of
clothes and jewels as if she were his own daughter.

It happened that one hot day Rhodopis was bathing in the
pool in her hidden garden. While she splashed in the cool
water her serving girls held her robe and her tiny, jewelled,
rose-red slippers. Suddenly an eagle swooped down out of
the sky. The serving girls dropped the robe and slippers
and fled in terror. But the eagle picked up one slipper in its
beak and flew off.

The sacred bird flew up the Nile to the Pharaoh's palace.
At that hour, Amasis was sitting in the great courtyard.
Down swooped the eagle and dropped the slipper into the
Pharaoh's lap.

Now Amasis was so delighted by the delicate slipper that
he felt sure the owner must be one of the most charming
girls in the land. So he sent forth messengers to find her,
declaring that the true owner should be his bride.

Soon the messengers came to Naucratis where they heard

tell of the beautiful Rhodopis. They visited Rhodopis and
found her in her garden by the side of the pool. She cried
out when she saw the slipper they carried for she knew that
it was hers.

So Rhodopis became Amasis' bride, and he made her his
Queen and Royal Lady of Egypt. And they reigned happily
together for the rest of their lives.

The pelican's problem

Mano lazed on the white sand and peeped through the stiff grass of the dunes. He watched the great waves rolling in from the ocean. Each one started off as deep blue and then it turned to light green and gold as it crashed on to the beach in the bright sunshine.

Suddenly, out of the corner of his eye, he saw something move and turning his head was surprised to see a strange bird standing beside him.

'Sorry, old chap,' squawked the bird, as Mano sprang up. 'I didn't mean to startle you.' He snapped his long beak together in a rat-a-tat-tat sound.

'I didn't know birds could talk,' said Mano, rubbing his eyes in wonder. 'And what sort of a bird are you, anyway?'

'Steady on!' said the bird. 'There's no need to be quite so surprised. I know I'm not much to look at, but as pelicans go, I'm told I cut quite a dash.'

Mano laughed as the pelican crossed his big orange feet and brushed a wing over the ragged feathers on his head.

'Trouble is,' the pelican went on, 'I was out there, swanning around, when I came over a bit strange. I really am ashamed to admit it, old man, but I get seasick, you know. All those waves going up and down are enough to turn a fellow off flying forever.'

'But what brings you to Portugal?' asked Mano. 'Where are you going?'

The pelican raised his eyebrows importantly. 'Meant to be going to Africa, actually,' he said. 'Big hot place down there.' He swung his beak towards the south. He hunched his shoulders. 'Gosh, I do feel sick.'

'Have you ever tried flying with your eyes shut?' asked Mano. 'Then you wouldn't see the waves.'

The bird stretched his long neck. 'What a good idea. I never thought of that.' His beak snapped into a long grin. 'And,' he chuckled, 'us birds are supposed to know where we're going blindfold, aren't we?' He chuckled even more. He flapped awkwardly into the air and flew around Mano's head. 'It works!' he squawked. 'Bye for now, old chap.'

Mano laughed out loud and waved. 'Bye,' he called.

'Rat-a-tat-tat, old boy,' said the pelican and he was gone.

Heart's desire

Many years ago, along the west coast of South America, lived the Inca people. Their empire was rich and proud and they had many temples and palaces of gold.

One day the king's son, Huayna, was in the palace courtyard, his golden shield in his hands. He was unhappy because it had been arranged for him to marry a stranger. 'I would much rather be using this shield in battle,' he thought, 'than wed!'

The shield flashed in the sun, and suddenly he remembered the old legend that if you lit the eyes of the Sun God, you would achieve your heart's desire. Huayna's desire was to lead the Inca Army!

The forbidden temple of the Sun God was high in the mountains, and a long climb. Inside was great splendour. Everywhere was gold, and above the golden altar, loomed the huge idol, with his staring, diamond eyes.

Huayna knelt before it, then caught a ray of sun from the window on his shield. Sure enough, the eyes flashed!

A door opened, and a beautiful girl entered. 'Why are you here?' she gasped, 'I am the bride of Huayna, and must not be seen.'

He was filled with great joy. 'I am Huayna,' he replied, and he realized that here, after all, was his heart's desire.

146

The magic clogs

'My feet are falling off!' said Anneke, the little Dutch girl.

Her brother, Johanne laughed. 'Nonsense! Just keep walking, or we'll be late for school again,' and he dragged Anneke along.

Windmills whirled in the sunshine and bright tulips glowed in the fields, but Anneke did not notice. Her feet hurt too much.

Some more children came dashing up and laughed at her. 'Baby-Cannot-Walk!' they called. 'Come, Johanne, you must leave her, then perhaps she will learn!'

So Johanne went with them. Tears filled Anneke's eyes. She wandered into a tulip field and sat down and cried.

Then, in between her tears, she suddenly noticed a pair of red clogs, peeping beneath the flower leaves. She stared with surprise, and picked them up.

What lovely, bright red clogs – not like her shabby, old ones! She tried them on, and they fitted perfectly. She couldn't believe it. But the most amazing thing was, her feet did not hurt any more.

'They must be magic clogs!' she laughed, dancing round the tulips. Then she set off and ran all the way to school.

The Bay of Smokes

Two thousand years ago, there was no one living in Iceland. The Vikings of Norway had discovered the island on one of their long voyages and it was they who called it Iceland because it was a land where there seemed to be nothing but ice and snow. The Vikings could not be bothered with such a strange, cold land.

At that time, there were many kings and chieftains in Norway. One of the kings, named Harald, wanted to marry a beautiful girl called Gydda, but she would not marry him unless he was the ruler of all Norway. At last Harald overcame all his rivals and Gydda became his wife. He continued to rule by force and declared that any chieftains who would not obey him would have to leave Norway.

Ingolfur Arnason was one chieftain who did not want to be ruled by Harald. He had been to Iceland before and knew no one would bother to follow him. So he decided to go back there. In the year 874, he left Norway with about four

hundred people who also wanted to get away from Harald
and had decided to make Iceland their home.

They had a long journey across rough seas to get to
Iceland, so, as was the custom then, they took with them
offerings to the gods that they might be granted a safe
voyage.

As their boats sailed nearer to the coast of Iceland,
Ingolfur threw his beautifully carved wooden throne
overboard. At the same time, he asked the gods to send the
throne ashore at a place where they could land. The boats
followed the throne until it drifted gently into a bay and
was washed on to the shore.

The boats landed safely but the Vikings were amazed to
see smoke rising into the air nearby. How could there be
fires when there were no people living there? They hoped
no other settlers had already taken the land.

Then they discovered that it was not smoke they could
see but steam. It rose from hot water bubbling out of the
depths of the earth. The Vikings were astounded – imagine
hot water flowing out of this icy earth!

So the Vikings found that Iceland was not such a cold
land after all and they called that place the Bay of Smokes.
And the town that was built there was called the same name,
which in Icelandic is Reykjavik. That town is now the
capital city of Iceland, and the hot springs, called geysers,
still bubble to this day.

The straw hat

Once upon a time in Japan there lived an old man and his wife. They were very poor and when New Year's Eve came around they found they had nothing in the house with which to celebrate the holiday.

They looked in all the cupboards, they shook out their rice-sacks, they emptied every box in the house and searched all over their tiny garden but they couldn't find even one grain of rice or one shred of cabbage. All they found was an old straw hat.

'Perhaps we could sell the hat,' said the old man, looking at it rather doubtfully.

'There is nothing else to sell,' said his wife, sadly.

So the two of them put on their warmest clothes (which were not very warm) and set off to the town.

It was snowing fast as they wandered the streets of the town crying, 'Hat for sale. Who will buy our straw hat!'

The few people out on such a bitter night looked at the couple as though they were mad. Who on earth would want

a straw hat on a cold New Year's Eve!

At last the husband and wife stopped and looked at each other. 'It's no good,' they said and they turned to trudge home. The snow was by now so thick that they could barely see where they were going. All at once the old man cried out in pain. 'I've stubbed my toe on something very hard,' he said, rubbing his foot crossly.

His wife peered through the whirling snowflakes. 'It is a stone statue of Jizo,' she cried. 'He is the guardian of children and travellers. Look how the snow has covered his face.' And taking the straw hat she put it gently on the statue's head. 'There,' she said, 'the hat has brought us no luck, maybe Jizo can make use of it. At least it will shelter his face from the snow.'

The two hurried on and at last reached their poor home. They had to go to bed cold and hungry.

Soon after they had at last fallen asleep they were woken by a loud thud outside the door. Looking out they saw a great sack full of food and, hurrying away, they saw a large, snow-covered, stone statue with a straw hat on his head. . . .

The ordinary antelope

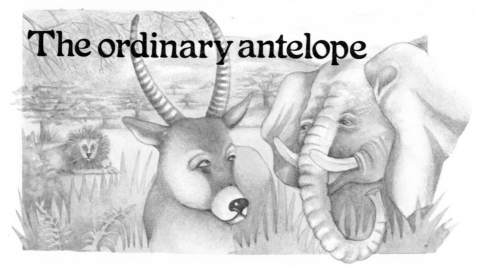

Antelope lived in a wildlife park in Kenya. Lots of people on holiday drove through the park and stopped to take photographs of the lions and giraffes and elephants.

'It's not fair,' said Antelope. 'Why doesn't anyone want to take a picture of me?'

'Because you're not interesting like us,' said Giraffe. 'Why, people like to look at me because I'm so tall, and Elephant because he's so big and Lion because he's so handsome. You – well, there's nothing very interesting about an antelope.'

Antelope became very upset. How could he make himself more interesting? He began to leap and dance about in front of the holidaymakers' cars but no one took any notice.

'What on earth are you doing, Antelope?' asked Elephant.

Antelope told him and Elephant chuckled so much his whole body shook. 'You're mad,' he said. 'Do you think it's *nice* to be stared at and pointed at all day? Why, I can't even give my back a quiet scratch without someone taking a photograph.'

Antelope thought about this for a while. Then he said, 'You're right, Elephant. How stupid I've been.' And, giving a leap of joy, Antelope galloped off across the park.

Sausage-eating

Walter was very excited. He lived in Munich and today was the first day of *Fasching*. All over Germany people celebrated during *Fasching*, for it was a carnival to mark the end of winter and the coming of spring. And in Munich they had Walter's favourite *Fasching* game – the sausage-eating contest! Walter was a rather greedy boy and loved sausages.

The winner of the competition was the person who ate the most sausages. The sausages were in a long string and two people ate the string, one at each end!

At last it was time for the contest to begin. Walter stood holding one end of the sausage string, glaring at his opponent and waiting for the starting bell to ring.

'Gulp!' Walter swallowed one sausage. 'Gulp!' Another gone. 'Gulp! Gulp! Gulp!'

But then the buttons burst off Walter's suit, one by one. And 'R-r-rip!' The seams on Walter's suit burst apart.

Well, Walter had won. But he was rolling on the ground, he felt so ill. And he had to go on a diet – you can be sure it didn't include sausages!

Mehdi's new home

Mehdi Mouse lived in Morocco, and he was looking for a new home. His last home had been in a friendly mule's stable, where Mehdi had done odd jobs in return for a comfortable straw bed. But the mule had got too old to work, and so the man who owned him bought a camel instead. The camel was very bad-tempered and hadn't liked Mehdi one bit. Twice he had tried to kick him.

Which was why Mehdi was looking for a new home. Thinking that there would be plenty of homes for mice in a big city, he decided to go to Tangier. But the people there didn't seem to like mice very much, and kept shooing him away.

After hunting around for several days, Mehdi found the perfect place – inside a mosque. It was quiet and cool in there and very grand, with a smooth marble floor and a fountain in the courtyard where Mehdi could have his morning wash. When the people came to worship in the mosque, Mehdi politely went for a walk. He soon grew very fond of his new home.

One day, he got back early from his walk and overheard a group of men talking. 'We can't possibly allow a mouse to live in our mosque,' said one man.

'No,' said another. 'We must get rid of him.'

Mehdi hid in the shadows, his whiskers trembling. What could he do to make himself useful so that they wouldn't mind him living there?

The next day he noticed that all the people who were worshipping in the mosque had left their shoes in a row outside. This was his chance! Quick as a flash he began to polish the shoes with his tail and whiskers.

He hadn't quite finished when the people started to come out of the mosque. When they saw a row of sparkling shoes, and Mehdi polishing away, they were all delighted, and everyone agreed that Mehdi could make his home in the mosque, after all.

The new hotel

Manuel lived with his father close to the sea in Spain. Each morning he would get up early to collect driftwood from the shore. He loved the feel of the warm, white sand between his toes and sometimes spent longer on the beach than he should have.

One morning he had not gone far when he walked right into a high wire fence. It stretched right across the beach and completely blocked his way. On it was a sign which said, 'Keep out – Hotel being built'.

He ran home and told his father what he had seen. Manuel's father was very angry and, putting on his best hat, he set off to see the hotel owners. When he returned he looked very sad. 'We can no longer use the beach,' he said. 'They have bought it for the hotel guests.'

The next morning, very early, there was a knock at the door. Two men, looking very important, stood on the step. One had a cross face and the other, who had an armful of

papers, looked upset.

Manuel's father invited them into the house. The cross
man smiled and his face seemed to vanish behind a huge row
of teeth. 'Dear sir,' he began, 'It seems we have . . . er . . .,'
he paused and scowled at his companion who promptly
dropped all his papers. 'We have,' he continued, 'built our
hotel on the wrong beach and now we discover that we have
no water supply.'

Manuel's father stood quietly thinking for a moment.
Then, with a twinkle in his eye, he said, 'I have a spring in
my garden, if that's any help to you.'

He led the two men out on to the porch in front of the
house. The three men talked for a long time but Manuel
couldn't hear a word. At last his father came back inside. He
was smiling. 'We can still use the beach,' he said. 'And in
return for water from the spring you can also have free
lemonade when the hotel opens!'